Death of a Chieftain

John Montague was born in Brooklyn, New York, and raised in Co. Tyrone. He is an internationally renowned poet and writer whose collections of poetry include *The Rough Field* (1972), *The Dead Kingdom* (1984), *Mount Eagle* (Gallery, 1989), and, most recently, *Collected Poems* (Gallery, 1995). His prose works include *The Lost Notebook* (Mercier, 1987), which received the first Hughes Award for fiction and *A Love Present and Other Stories* (Wolfhound, 1997). The musical group The Chieftains took its name from the title story of *Death of a Chieftain and Other Stories*. John Montague was appointed the first Ireland Professor of Poetry in 1998. He lives in West Cork and in New York.

By the Same Author

Poetry
Poisoned Lands (1961)
A Chosen Light (1967)
Tides (1970)
The Rough Field (1972)
A Slow Dance (1975)
The Great Cloak (1978)
Selected Poems (1982)
The Dead Kingdom (1984)
Mount Eagle (1988)
Time in Armagh (1993)
Collected Poems (1995)

Anthologies
The Faber Book of Irish Verse (1974)
Bitter Harvest (1989)

Fiction
A Love Present & Other Stories (1997)

Essays
The Figure in the Cave (1989)

Death of a Chieftain

& Other Stories

John Montague

WOLFHOUND PRESS

This edition published 1998 by
Wolfhound Press Ltd
68 Mountjoy Square
Dublin 1, Ireland
Tel: (353-1) 874 0354
Fax: (353-1) 872 0207

First published in 1964 by
MacGibbon & Kee Ltd.

Published 1978 by Poolbeg Press Ltd.

The Arts Council
An Chomhairle Ealaíon   Wolfhound Press receives financial assistance from The Arts Council/
An Chomhairle Ealaíon, Dublin, Ireland.

British Library Cataloguing in Publication Data
A catalogue record for this book is available from the British Library.

ISBN 0-86327-673-3

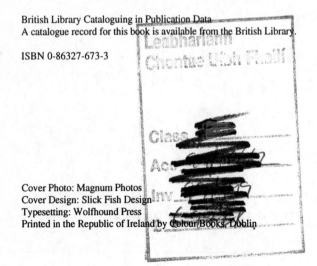

Cover Photo: Magnum Photos
Cover Design: Slick Fish Design
Typesetting: Wolfhound Press
Printed in the Republic of Ireland by Colour Books, Dublin

Contents

That Dark Accomplice

THE BOYS disliked him intensely, with his dark intolerant head, his way of walking as though contemptuous of stone and earth, they being merely the material on which he drew the unmistakable lines of his purpose. 'No nonsense', the proud tilt of that head seemed to say from the start, and recognising their master, as boys in a bulk nearly always do, they could still resent his mastery, as puppies resent sullenly the hand that makes them smart under the switch. Dislike? Was it anything as definite? Rather a vague resentment that forced its way towards expression through the long greyness of that Ulster winter term. Had you halted one of them, a shamefaced lad only broken to longers, dawdling by the ball-alley or kicking the scuffed grass of the Senior Ring slope with unpolished slackly-tied shoes, and asked him, point blank 'Why?' he would have been startled and lost, with nothing to say for himself except to mutter rebelliously that the new Dean was 'a brute'.

Which seemed to mean, in fact, only that the new Dean knew how to handle them too, too well, and strode the dormitories punctually in the cold mornings as the electric buzzers clattered harshly against the wall, his high voice giving strength to the hated Latin greeting, *Benedicamus Domino*, the flexible cane twitching at his soutane's edge.

'Up, you, sluggards! Little boys should be early birds. Come now, Johnson, don't fester in the bed-clothes.' The cane rattled along the rails of the bed, flicked against thin legs dancing at a line of washbasins. 'Come now, boys, all together now — *Deo Gratias*!' Dodging on bare soles over scrubbed board, or tumbling from warm bed-clothes, the boys mustered a weak, scattered reply: *Deo Gratias*. Oh! he could handle them, reducing their boyish pride to little more than a scamper out of the way of a stick.

It wasn't only the cold mornings that gave them reason for hatred, but the hundred other deliberately irritating ways in which he proved his authority. Naturally an independent, high-spirited man, he had spent his early priesthood in England where he quickly gained a reputation as a successful missioner and preacher. Then, one day, he found himself transferred from the pulpit and placed among schoolboys, unable to relax his trained arrogance, his emphatic rhetorical gestures, and too far from boyhood to appreciate its special gauche tenderness. Even his speech seemed alien, brusque and clear-cut, the exact opposite of the slurred speech of the boys and the other local priests, snuffling over Greek texts in Ulster accents and making pawky jokes that endeared them to successive generations of pupils. 'Corny', 'Chappie', 'Dusty'; those were nicknames that testified to familiarity, even love, but all they could think to call him, reaching out vainly for some image to equal their dislike, was 'Death's Head' or 'Hatchet'. 'He's a brute', and with that recognition, humanity, for them, dropped from his shoulders; he became someone who struck, and must in turn be struck, the problem being where or when or with what concerted violence.

In one small incident or another, he came to sense their hatred, but remained unperturbed; indeed, he seemed almost amused by it, as though waiting to pounce with joy on the first reflex of insubordination. It became his custom to speak to them on every possible occasion, after prayers, in the still moment before Grace, from his dais in the studyhall above their sullen heads. His vibrant tones rebuked, lectured, played with them, sent them running out with a kindly general pat of dismissal. Under the substance of his words, the breaking of some minor rule, the loss of rosary beads in the grounds, or the 'slovenly disgusting' habit of sticking hands to the wrist into tattered pockets, ran a nervous note of triumph that seemed to recognise the silent war declared against him, even to defy it. 'Try it, you little fools,' it seemed to say. 'I'll soon show you how to handle a pack of grimy schoolboys.' Yet, steadily they sensed in him, somewhere and not explicit, a weakness, a febrile excess of emotion that might, for all his outward show and insistence, leave him helpless in some extraordinary situation.

II

One Friday evening, Benediction ending with the Divine Praises and the restless chink of the thurible in an altar server's hand, four boys, older than the rest, left the school chapel early, tiptoeing down the aisle with lowered heads and out onto the yard between the lavatory and the disused air-raid shelters. They stood, rubbing their thighs nervously, looking across at the lit glass of the chapel windows, all opaque save one where a Virgin's dark-blue head curved tenderly over the slight cube of the Child's body.

'Much time left?' asked one.

'A few minutes.'

'Maybe we've time for a fag. I'm nearly dead for the want of one,' said the third, gesturing towards the lavatory door.

The boys generally smoked in the damp lavatory, twenty yards or so from the back of the sacristy, passing the butts under the wooden partitions or pretending to stand at the urinal where the tepid water gushed and leaked. At a moment's notice the hot end would hiss into the water, or turn alive against the palm as the hurrying Dean peered and prodded under the doors, or turned out the pockets of malingerers.

'Pah, this place reeks of smoke, stinks of it.' The cane would grate across the glass in the top half of a lavatory door, while inside a frightened boy cowered among white tiles, a cigarette dead under his foot, braces dangling down his back.

'Better not. He'll be here any minute now, and we're to give the word to start.'

'Shush! There's the first touch of the Adoremus.'

Inside the chapel, the congregation of boys rose for the last hymn, singing loudly and unevenly, and then subsided into their seats. Some craned rudely around to watch the priests rising from their prie-dieus: old Father Keane was, as usual, the last to leave, lifting his lame leg outwards and shuffling towards the door. Others prayed with averted heads, making a cage of their hands. On the high-altar the server dowsed the last candlelight and the nave of the chapel was heavy with incense and smoke from the fuming wicks. Restless with the thought of some strange excitement, the boys waited as the head-prefect went over to lock back the swinging doors. Then they came in a rush.

Supper always followed Friday Benediction, the refectory only thirty feet away, with rickety wooden stairs up to it, the space between like a platform onto which the boys poured. This evening they were unusually silent; the four boys who had been waiting outside the chapel now appeared a little way apart, up the corridor, lounging with their backsides against the wall, eyes alert. At the far end they saw the Dean approaching, a tall figure with billowing soutane, carrying himself proudly as if bearing the Sacrament. 'Right, boys, let him have it!' they called. Turning their faces to the wall, everyone booed, dragging air into distended mouths, and forcing it out through tightened twisted lips. Boo-o-o-o.

Half-way down the hall he stopped, head flinching backwards as though from a sudden blow across the mouth.

Watching intently, Tony Johnson, one of the four ringleaders, cried in excited confirmation: 'We have him, he's yellow.' The long harsh sound became stronger, gathering into itself all the suppressed vindictiveness of months and seeming to fill the area around the chapel door with the palpable presence of hatred.

Then, regaining confidence, he began to walk forward, but his eyes shielded slightly, his body in the exaggerated posture of a man under stress. The crowd opened before him. As the last students, timid boys with Holy Water damp on their foreheads, came pushing their way through the chapel door, having deliberately lingered to escape any possible punishment, he reached the foot of the stairs, and sprang into the refectory, two steps at a time. There was a moment of doubt and delay; the booing subsided: there were whispers of 'What'll we do now?' The bigger boys gave the lead, climbing after him into the barn-like refectory, filing according to age and class among the oil-clothed tables, with their regular mounds of loaf bread, white damp plates with a print of butter on each, and exactly arranged rows of chairs. There was the usual silence for Grace, all facing towards the end of the hall, where, directly over the Dean's bent head, the crucifix hung like a twisted root on the yellow wall. 'Bless us, O Lord, and these thy gifts . . .' the voice was steady but the hands perhaps a little too tightly joined. Chairs scraped on the linoleum as the boys settled into their places.

Any ordinary evening, after the hush of Grace, conversation broke out immediately, almost like an explosion. Now there was silence, dead, utter silence, as though someone had given a signal, or everyone been stuck dumb. The white-aproned country maids, grinning good-naturedly as they carted the big blue and red teapots to each table, looked around with surprise, hearing nothing but the rattle of knives, the chink of cups, the bodily shifting necessary in the sharing out of the tiers of white sliced bread: in the space above the moving hands and heads and the white cloth of the table covers, the air seemed to thicken with expectancy, as though every breath was being held too long, and the damp walls sweated.

A quarter of an hour passed without break. The meal was nearly over and the Dean had done nothing yet, fidgeting slightly before the dais, playing with the sleeves of his soutane, brushing them, looking at the chalk-smeared elbows. At the Senior tables the boys kept glowering around anxiously, hoping that he would do or say something, while the little boys shifted on their seats with half frightened excitement. He gave no hint of his feelings, however, appearing to turn the incident slowly over in his mind, meditating some unusual form of retaliation.

The boys began to feel uneasy; perhaps after all their action had been too hasty, presenting him only with a new cause for amusement? The unnatural atmosphere of silence, in a place which usually resounded with laughter and squabbling voices, strained their nerves to a jagged pitch. Perhaps indeed their action had been foolish, a glancing ugly blow that left him unharmed and put them even more at his mercy than before. The very silence they had created cut them off from further action, and his acceptance of it seemed to say with a shrug: 'All right, if that's the way you want it, then all the better for me. You can keep your silence to the crack of doom for all I care. You're only depriving yourselves.'

Suddenly, every startled eye upon him, the Dean began to walk up and down between the tables, his rubber soles squealing softly on the linoleum. Slowly at first, a thinking pace, with the head down; and then, as resolution formed, more swiftly. The nervous lengthy stride, parallel to the listening tables, now had its usual impulsive rhythm, the rhythm of a man whose mind was made up, who was confident he could master the situation. As he took a corner with almost theatrical swiftness and firmness, the soutane belling out like a skirt round his ankles, someone tittered. His head went up, with a sharp decisive movement. Far down, at one of the Junior tables, a boy sniggered helplessly into his teacup.

'You down there, O'Rourke. Was that you?'

He came hurrying towards the boy, now blubbering with fear and hysterical laughter. 'Was it you, I say? Have you no manners at all, man? Can't you speak up?'

'Yes, Father.'

'So it was!' Arms folded, he stood at the edge of the table. 'That's a pretty thing for a boy of your age to be at — sniggering behind backs like a schoolgirl. It's a pity we can't get you something better to do than that, isn't it?'

'Yes, Father.'

'Well, I know something that'll fit you better than sniggering. Do you see that book up there?' — he pointed towards the dais for reading during meals, usual only during Lent. 'You can go up there and keep us all edified with *The Lives of the Saints*.'

'Yes, Father.'

'I suppose you can read' — the voice came down low and sarcastic — 'and you all want to keep silence anyway so here's something to keep your little minds busy.'

The boy rose and scuttled towards the reading dais, the whole school watching him with stunned curiosity, while he searched eagerly for support in every face. Propped up high over all the wondering heads, a minute sulky figure, his ears red at the edges as though the flesh had been smartly slapped, his hands frantically turning the leaves, while a leaflet fell, swirling, to the floor:

'Hurry up, man, don't be so clumsy. You've got an audience, you know. We're all dying to hear you.'

'Where, Father?'

'Anywhere. We're waiting.'

'The life of the saintly Vicaire d'Arcueil teaches us this lesson: that the true way of sanctity lies in an infinite gentleness and patience with all human follies, all human wickedness. We must expel from our rebellious hearts every taint of self before we can hope to see God. As a seminarian, he was ridiculed for his ignorance of Latin, his peasant clumsiness. As a sanctified priest, he was mocked by his parishioners, who found him naive . . .'

The Dean was enjoying his part now, playing it to perfection, almost a Mephistopheles in dark deliberate position, mouth tilted and sardonic, foot tip-tapping restlessly as he leaned back at an angle against the foodpresses, under the crucifix. A kind of grim contentment arched his eyebrows; he seemed to savour every mispronunciation with intense interest, gloating over every slur and stutter — and there were many, the boy on the reading dais stopping and starting, squirming and shifting — till he could no longer contain his great mirth.

'Good Lord, man, higher.'

'And yet for the forty years of his ministry, he moved through the parish of Arcueil like a ministering angel . . .'

'Louder, boy, louder. Is that the best you can do? Is there a stone in your throat, or were you never taught to read?'

'Please, Father, there are too many big words,' the boy wailed, his fingers hot and fumbling the pages, his timid eyes pleading for release. O'Rourke was an awkward lout at any time, the kind of boy who, through sheer lack of even the most ordinary schoolboy cunning, was always caught out in mischief, or found himself left behind to bear the blame after his more cute companions had skipped aside. And yet nothing pleased him more than to be thought daring and impudent, scuttling around the edge of a crowd with a vehement conspiratorial air or trying to catch the limelight in class by loud words and laughs. Knowing his victim of old, the Dean now played him with all the nervous mockery he could command, goading the boy till he stammered like an idiot.

'Open your mouth, man. Wider!'

'This humble man had learnt the ways of charity, that sweet radiance of the Christian soul which is our best weapon against evil. Conceit, egotism, pride, all the diverse and unsuspected ways of selfishness were alien to him; as though by dint of prayer he had driven that dark accomplice forever from his bosom . . .'

'*Booosom*. Is that the best you can do?' the Dean intoned down his nose, making the word sound broad as a snore. Driven past all enduring, O'Rourke collapsed into a flood of tears, weeping with great ugly shudders, as though the breath was tearing out the softer part of his throat. The Dean looked stunned; a faintly comic amazement made his mouth gape open like a fish. From every corner of the refectory, low but insistent, a growing undertone to the boy's abandoned sobbing, came again the sound of booing.

'Leave him alone,' someone called, 'leave him alone.'

He pulled himself up as though trying to escape the accusing sound, as though suddenly very weary.

'Boys,' he began uncertainly, striving to get away into some kind of speech that might right the balance, administer remorse. 'Boys, you have done something this day which I had not expected of you and which I will not forget for a long time to come. I have tried to keep silent, to pass the matter off as a joke, but if you are not careful it will go too far, and I will be compelled to put the whole matter in other hands.'

'Boys,' groaned a wag sepulchrally, from a corner. The whole school laughed madly, beating the spoons against the cups, the plates against the wood, jangling the gross enamel teapots. Above the tintinnabulation, his voice strove to be heard, no longer exact and peremptory, but high and nervous, falteringly demanding an audience, almost a whinny.

'You are too young perhaps to know what duty means. You do not know how hard it had been for me to play this unpleasant role of Dean. But since it is my duty, I have tried to do it well, though it is the last thing I would have chosen for myself. I'm not good tempered, perhaps — I may have seemed unduly harsh to you — and I may have made mistakes — but I have tried to be conscientious. Do you think I like to be shut up with schoolboys day after day, watching their every whim . . .'

At first they listened, struck by a note of sincerity in his voice; then, ceasing to understand, recognised only the familiar smoothness, the intellectual fibre of the words that was so hateful to them. As they began again their systematic interruption, he lost all self-control and began to rail.

'You have chosen to show your hatred for me in the only way you know — that of booing. It is entirely typical. But I'm not afraid to face it, I can tell you. I can take it. You might have scared someone else with your Nazi hysterics, but I can take it.'

His own image, no longer proud and disdainful, but crushed and reduced, returned to him openly from every grinning, gesticulating face. Seized by something like the impersonal frenzy of the hunting pack, no longer single ordinary boys, hiding their hatred behind barred fingers, they rocked back and forward in moaning laughter, hooting and cawing and quacking.

'I can take it, boys,' squeaked someone in a high feminine voice.

The Dean's face flushed and for a moment he seemed to resist the temptation to lift the cane and plough madly among the tables, striking everyone indiscriminately. But he would have had to flail half the school and the big boys might easily have struck back, made reckless by their hatred and conscious of their advantage in numbers. The dangerous aloofness which had been his power was now swept away from him; he was no longer a priest or a person in authority, but merely someone who had humbled and hurt another past enduring.

Almost crying, he tried to raise his voice above the noise: 'Do you know what you have done? Is there no limit for you at all? Boo me if you like, it makes no difference now. But tonight you have booed me, a priest before the very chapel door. You didn't think of that, did you? No one can forgive you for that, neither I nor anyone else.'

There was a sudden silence. He had played his last, best, and forgotten card, facing their monstrous grinning abandon with his outraged cloth. This was an appeal none of the boys had anticipated, a transference of their insult to the person of Christ himself. And in a moment they knew it was false, that he had only thought of it as a weapon to protect his injured egotism.

'You might have chosen some more suitable place for your hoodlum demonstrations. Has education taught you nothing better than that?' Refreshed, he felt the silence, guessed that his words had shocked them back to their senses, restored his shrunken image. 'Imagine, for a group of boys from good Catholic homes . . .'

At one of the three Senior tables, someone belched: a deliberate vulgar sound. The school shrieked with merriment. The sound was repeated on thick burbling lips, from every table in the hall. The Dean stumbled in his words as though shot; he fumbled and lost the thread of his argument and then let his head slip into his hands, seeking darkness in the warm shelter of his palms.

The head-prefect rose hurriedly and said Grace. The Dean did not look up, though it was normally he who announced the end of a meal.

'We give thee thanks, O Almighty God . . .'

Quietly and in perfect order the boys filed out between the tables. The winter mist had filled the corners of the large refectory windows, making them look like show cases. Going out, one or two looked closely at the Dean, without sympathy but with a detached curiosity. He was weeping silently. He looked like a man either drunk or sick, his back humped and his shoulders slack as though props had been taken away and the cloth sagged without support. 'Go away,' he said, without raising his head. 'Can't you go away!' The last clumped down the stairs, leaving the Dean alone, except for the boy on the dais who had stopped whimpering to watch him. 'Go away,' he said, sensing somebody still near. O'Rourke rose and scuttled towards the door.

Outside the evening was cold, softly growing darker, the ball-alleys a great grey bulk without separate outline. In the town below, the lights were coming on, despite the blacked out windows, vague points against the winter mist. The damp air was threatening; another night of rain would drown the playing fields and turn the slopes into a sea of mud. Already, around the Senior Ring, moist drops hung like grain from the naked branches.

The boys scattered with wild and joyous cries.

The New Enamel Bucket

WHEN JOHN Rooney left his home to go to the fair in Moorhill he meant to be back early. It was spring and there was a lot to be done, from ploughing late fields to sowing early ones. Beside, he had to do all the work now himself: his father was too old to do more than complain, watching behind the window-blind all day to see that his son did not slacken, or hobbling along the margin of a field to judge if the furrows were straight. As John rose to lift his cap from a nail, his father glared at him: 'What do you want to go hightailing to town for anyway?' he said peevishly. 'Do you think the fair won't get on without you? Nothing but outings for the young nowadays: fit you better to stay at home.' And as he passed through the scullery door, his mother called after him, raising her head from the bucket of hen's meat she was preparing: 'Mind, now, don't make your stay too long.'

He got his bicycle, an ancient Raleigh with truncheon handlebars, from the turfshed, where it was propped up against an old spraying barrel. A flock of chickens scattered from under his feet as he mounted with a slow but stately movement. Moorhill was only a few miles away, first down the lane and then along the country road which ran towards Enniskillen. He took the lane slowly, for the surface was uneven: now and again one of the wheels hopped and bumped on a big stone and he cursed under his breath. At last he swung out, with relief, onto the tarred surface of the main road, and began pedalling vigorously towards town.

John Rooney was in his early thirties, a little over six foot in height, with large hands, weak blue eyes, and a long nose.

He always wore a cap, with the peak pulled rakishly over one eye, in imitation of a Gaelic footballer he had once seen, famous for his burly viciousness. But in reality he was a quiet, gentle person, passive by nature: 'John Rooney's a good sort,' people said, without enthusiasm, as though speaking of some placid cow or sheep. As he cycled, he observed with interest the land on either side, the chug of a Ford tractor crossing a headland, crows converging on the steely-black of a new furrow, beneath the dark line where the heather began, like the fringe of a scalp. In former times, the Black Mountain district had been known for its highwaymen, outlawed Catholics whose farms had been seized, but there was nothing to remind one of that today. It was a fresh, sunny morning and everything seemed pleasantly relevant: birds darted in the spring hedgerows and the freewheel of his bicycle sang on the gentle descent of the mountain road.

As he approached Moorhill, he began to overtake knots of cattle being driven to the fair. Most of the men were from his own area, dressed in the half-style of towngoing attire, a good coat worn with overalls or other working clothes. He nodded to them soberly as he passed, a swift sideways dip of the head indicating recognition and greeting. Among them was his nearest neighbour, Willy Boyle, or 'Long Willy' as the countryside called him, with cheerful misanthropy, because he was only five foot in height. Willy was driving two heifers in front of him, shouting energetically as he thumped their backs with a sally rod: 'Up there, you bastards, yup there.'

John Rooney had never been a close friend of Willy's but he believed in being a good neighbour, so he drew in to accompany him, letting his legs dangle from the pedals.

''Lo, Willy.'

''Lo, John, how's the farm? For the fair?'

'Might stay an hour or so. You should do well with them beasts.'

'I could do well and I could do nothing at all. Depends on the bloody dealers!'

'Them's good animals, though. If the one on the outside takes after her mother she'll be a great wee milker.'

The cow in question, a sleek brown polly with soft white markings, like splashes of paint, made a sudden dart for an open gap. As Willy rushed after it with violent oaths, John Rooney drove his bicycle forward, interposing the front wheel to block the heifer's path.

'In the nick. I'll be moving on now, Willy.'

'Abyssinia, John.'

'See you, Willy.'

Moorhill consisted of one long main street, originally used as the fairground, and a rabbit warren of side streets, where cottages crumbled into sad disorder. Seen from the narrow-gauge railway, or the lofty new by-pass of the main road, it gave an impression of extreme bleakness: the huddled grey backs of the houses, festooned with piping, looked mortuary. In the border area of Ulster, cut off from its natural southern hinterland, there were generally two sorts of towns: the surviving and the slack. But Moorhill was more than slack, it was stagnant, which was partly responsible for its peculiar reputation among its neighbours. 'I was never married,' people would say with relish at the mention of its name, 'but I was twice in Moorhill.'

There had only been one attempt at an industry within living memory: the stump of a dead linen mill dominated the centre of the town like a funeral monument. Under the system of social relief developed by His Majesty's post-war government, extreme poverty had passed, but there was still an aura of raffishness, a down-at-heel quality about Moorhill. The town remained sharply divided between the middle-class (professional people, merchants, publicans) whose main income came from the countryside, and the unemployed whose quarrels received vivid reports in the rather biased local paper produced in the county seat, twenty miles away. Of late, there had been some agitation to improve the housing, but the town's reputation, and the consequent uneasy belligerence of its supporters had prevented much progress: it still remained, according to a County Councillor, 'one of the dirtiest wee towns in the North of Ireland'. He was referring to the plumbing and was lobbying for its improvement, but when he next passed through Moorhill his remark was remembered: he found a dead dog and a brimming household utensil in the back seat of his parked car. In its fiercely defensive patriotism, Moorhill found it hard to distinguish friend from foe.

John Rooney drove his bicycle slowly up Main Street until he reached the embattled virgin of the Boer War Monument. On one side of the street was a bar, The Mountain Rest, which belonged to a family which had originally came from Black Mountain; it was there John generally left his bicycle. He wheeled it down the piss-sour entry into an old shed and then came through the back door of the house into the bar. He ordered a bottle of stout and stood drinking near the window, through which he was able to see the early business of the fair, a cart passing with a load of pigs, an old clothes man setting up his stall. Now and again he turned to speak to the barman, a lean young fellow in a spotted sportshirt.

'How'd your bitch do in the trials?'

'You never saw anything like it. She ate the track.'

'If she hits that form in Belfast you'll be all right.'

'I'll be made.'

'Is she as good a goer as Moorhill Lass?'

Moorhill Lass was a famous greyhound, bred by the same man, which had reached the final of the Balmoral Cup only a few years before. Its prowess had already passed into local mythology and various forms of foul play on the part of the city people were held responsible for its downfall.

'She sights the hare better, a better starter, like. You should see her shoot from that trap, man, like a bloody bullet. But she's bad on the bends, comes too wide. And she's very easy upset, finicky, you know. The least wee thing puts her off her food.'

'It's the breeding makes them nervous.'

There was silence for a few moments. John gazed deeply through the window and the barman busied himself behind the counter, arranging empties.

'Are you for buying, the day?' the barman asked finally, for civility's sake.

'Naw. No grazing left. But I still like to come in for a look round me.'

'Nothing like a fair,' said the barman, without conviction: he obviously regarded the countryside as an inexplicable hangover from the days before the invention of the internal combustion engine.

'People say the move to the Commons has spoiled it.'

'Ah, I dunno, we do the same business only later and longer.'

'Well, good-bye now.'

'Maybe you'll be by again.'

'Hardly. There's a lot to be done at home and I can't stay more than an hour or so.'

'Good luck, anyway.'

As John Rooney passed out through the door, the barman reached for his glass and rinsed it under the tap. Countrymen were all right, but God, some of them were a fearful drag. If his bitch won, maybe he should move to Belfast and get a job in a really flash bar, with a lounge and all the latest: his mother could easily do without him for a while. Then he could take out that big blonde he had met in the Club Orchid: she had headlights on her like a Transport lorry. She might get more than she expected, and better than she thought, if his boat came in. Through the window he saw a group crossing the street towards The Mountain Rest: business was slow but it was beginning.

The hands of the courthouse clock registered midday as John Rooney walked down the street towards the Commons, the large stretch of wasteland between the cinema and the railway yard, which had recently been taken over as a fairground. The fair was now in full session: cattle bawled mournfully and pigs raced squealing around wooden pens, where buyers leaned ceremoniously over to inspect them, scratching their scaly backs with ashplants. A sow and her litter lay exposed in the crate of a cart, the piglets burrowing with blind fury into the pink recumbent body of their mother: now and again, one tottered to its feet and rooted for a better position. Children out for their play-hour darted through the pens and the carts, and around the great wheels of the cattle lorries. From a public house near the fairground came the nasal twang of a ballad singer.

John pushed his way through the throng, halting every now and then to appraise a beast, or watch a bargain being made. Within a ring of onlookers, two men faced each other, hats pulled low, ashplants stuck under their armpits like swagger sticks. The object of their contest, a large heifer, stood sullenly between them, swishing its tail over its fly-spotted flanks. A third man broke through the spectators with massive authority, just as the prospective buyer was turning away in an elaborate mime of disgust. Seizing a hand of each he brought them together in a reluctant banging of palms: 'Now, John Kelly, you and Tommy Drummond are both decent men; you wouldn't let a few pennies stand between you. Split the differ and the bargain's made: are you game, Kelly?'

John Rooney savoured the scene with deep satisfaction. The ritual bargaining always gave him great pleasure, although it was on the way out, now that the cattle-dealers had become so strong, smooth middle-men who went from fair to fair and knew the ways of the world, how to keep prices down, where and when to ship. And the move to the Commons had taken away a good deal of the interest in the fair, though people said it might end well if the cattle-marts took over. But hand to hand bargaining was what John Rooney knew best, secret ploys and approaches passed on to him by his father while he was still a gaping boy. It was one of the reasons why he had come to the fair, that and the vague urge for a little company after the lonely weeks working in the mountain fields. But today he wished to remain uninvolved; whenever he was asked to give his judgement on an animal, he was careful to speak only in platitudes, and if anyone tried to enmesh him as mediator to complete a noisy deal, he managed to escape. 'Not today, James,' or 'I have to be going soon,' accompanied by elaborate shrugs of self-depreciation, butting his cap sideways at the air: 'Naw, naw, not now.'

But the lowing of the cattle, the strong sour reek of dung and old clothes, so many familiar sights and sounds soothed him, like a drug. Meeting a neighbour from Black Mountain, they would fall into an attitude of interest like two crows on a paling wire. The sun had begun to move down the sky before he finally turned to leave the fairground. As he plodded reluctantly up Main Street, he heard somebody calling him: 'Hello there, John Rooney, you long streak of misery, you.' It was Willy Boyle, his hat set back on his tiny head at a jaunty angle, his face lit with excitement and compulsive goodwill. He saluted John in a derisive whine:

'Lord, some people are in the tearing hurry! Are you going to walk right past a neighbour and not ask him if he had a mouth on him at all?'

'Hello, there, Willy, I was just heading home.'

'What hell hurry's on you? Sure it's only a while since you passed me on the Black Mountain road. It's long till bedtime.'

'I have to be home,' said John uneasily, but his companion was not even listening.

'Do you know how much I got for them,' said he excitedly, digging a bundle of notes from his pocket. 'Go on, guess.' But before John could hazard a figure, he blurted out his news: 'Sixty pound . . . and I declare to God me only counting on fifty.'

'You had luck the day all right,' said John, eyeing the bundle of notes under his nose with appropriate approval.

'I had luck all right,' said Willy, grudgingly, 'but I had something more important: a good sharp eye in me head. Come in to Donnelly's now to christen this handful, and I'll tell you the whole story.'

John Rooney looked at the little man with some apprehension. His eyes were slightly red-rimmed and he spoke very rapidly: it was obvious that he already had a few drinks in him and was ready for more. He had a new bucket looped over his arm, a white enamel bucket of the kind used in the country for carrying spring water: it gave him a gipsy look.

'Honestly, Willy, I'd rather not. I told them at home I'd be back to do a bit of ploughing before evening.'

'Ach, hold your horses, man. One drink won't harm you. Sure I have to get home myself, and I have more to carry than you.' He tapped the wad of notes significantly. 'Come on, now, and stop dragging. Isn't it a terrible thing when your own

country man won't drink good fortune with you and you have
to spend your money on strangers?'

Reluctant, John surrendered: an appeal to local patriotism
was too final to reject. He did not object to drinking with the
little man, but Boyle had the reputation of being troublesome
when he had drink taken. Yet if he only stayed for a round or
two there would be no harm done and he would still be home
in time for a late dinner.

'OK Willy, just the one for old time's sake and to christen,
your bargain.'

'That's the man. You can take me home with you when
you're going and we'll both be the one road. Right?'

By evening the main street was quiet, the few clothes dealers dismantling their stalls, an occasional straggle of cattle
passing through on their way home, unsold. 'There's old Clemens driving home his three stirks,' said Willy Boyle, looking
through the window of the public house. 'God, but they're the
right hungry creatures. You'd think they never saw a pick of
grass in their born days.'

'They're not too fat, indeed.'

'Fat! Ye could nearly walk through them. If he wasn't too
bloody mean to feed them he'd have done better today. But
they were always a close pack in Castleisland anyway.'

'Easy on,' whispered John Rooney into Willy's ear.
'There's a neighbour of Clemens, Big Tom Jackson, over there
drinking in the corner.'

'What do I care about Tom Jackson,' said Willy, pushing
John's hand away. 'Do you think I give one damn. I was only
saying what everyone knows, that Clemen's cattle are no
bloody good.'

'All right, Willy, you're right enough. Drink up your stout
and we'll be going.'

'Going me ass. There's time for a few yet. And if you don't have the money, I'm the boy can do the trick.'

Staggering slightly on his pigeon-frail legs, Willy Boyle reached into his inside pocket and drew out the soiled bundle of banknotes. He waved them at arm's length above his head, like a victorious boxer posing for applause.

'Do you see that, men? You never saw a Boyle yet without money to stand his turn.'

The group of men in the corner, towards whom Willy Boyle was ostentatiously addressing his remarks, were from the rich farming district of Castleisland, on the far side of Black Mountain, towards Lough Erne. Large-headed, colonial, calm as the plump animals they bred, the Castleisland men chewed the cud of their conversation, without paying much attention to the other people in the pub, although once or twice Tom Jackson gave Willy a sharp, half-amused glance. Their indifference angered the little man, who was now pretty far gone, and spoiling for a fight. In their refusal to take him seriously, he scented their poor opinion of him, as though he were no more than a bluebottle buzzing in the window. He struck the counter with his fist, making the glasses jump.

'I'm fit to buy a drink with any man here. Isn't that right, barman?' he queried, shoving his face, with its uneasy ferret's eyes, fiercely forward. 'What hell pub are we in, anyway?'

Since their meeting at three o'clock, he and John Rooney had been in several, beginning with the one nearest the fairground, and then working their way up the street in illogical order, from the Dew Drop Inn, to the Corner House, to the Sunshine Bar, until they reached the one where John had left his bicycle, The Mountain Rest. There they had been for over an hour, during which time John had made many proposals to leave for home. Willy, who was now at the stage when he spilled half his drink in raising it to his mouth, was still determined, as he said (with a leer towards the corner to stress his mocking use of the old Orangeman's war-cry) to move 'not an inch'. John was relatively sober, most of his energy being taken up, not with drinking, but with trying to keep the little man out of rows; but the noise, the lack of food and the anxiety were beginning to tell on him: his head felt heavy and his eyes ached with smoke. He made another appeal, *sotto voce*.

'Right now, Willy, drink up and we'll hit the road. I'd like to see you bring that wad home safe, as well as yourself.'

'Ah, damn your drink up. Won't we be at home for the rest of our lives. Home was never like this.'

'I know all that, Willy, but there's some boys about this town would skin you as fast as look at you.'

John Rooney looked anxiously around him as he spoke to see if his remark had been overheard. In his triumphal progress up the street, Willy had accumulated quite a few hangers-on, whose eyes glistened at the sight of his much waved bundle of banknotes. For one of the characteristics of Moorhill was the number of 'gentleman of leisure' it supported: stray unemployed in whom the pristine loss of pride at being without steady work or craft had been perverted into a systematic delight in living on their wits. The dole gave them barely enough to live on, but nothing to fill their empty hours. Generally, they were to be seen against the courthouse wall, where their shoulders had traced a wavering line of grime. But they could smell free drink as bees smell honey from one side of a field to another, and their system of communication was highly developed. The leader was big Andy Cleggan, who wore a raft-like straw hat from which ribbons dangled. As a boy he had been clever beyond the average, and his fond parents had sent him to college, hoping to turn him into a white collar worker; but he fell promptly to the bottom of every job and by the time he had decided to reform, it was already too late. He had lost his last job, driving an oil tanker, three years before, when he crashed into a tree outside Lisburn. Beside him was Jimmy the Jail, whose thirst derived from the dimly remembered horrors of the Flanders campaign. A stonemason, from a long line of stonemasons, he had emerged shell-shocked and spent, with shaking hands. When his pension was done, he would take to drinking methylated spirits or turpentine; his pockets were littered with tiny bottles, sold illegally for a shilling or two, which gave off a sickly sweet odour. He had even been known, *in extremis*, to drink boot polish: long periods in jail, sewing mail bags, had not eased his longing for oblivion, in whatever form. There was 'Dandy' MacHugh, who dressed carefully in a natty grey suiting, indeterminate in age, but with razor-edge creases, brown brogues with a Celtic design toecap, and a checked golfer's cap. There was a clothes salesman called Black Barney, whose speech was so slurred as to be almost meaningless: he wore a bright red shirt, a tattered black hat and army surplus fatigues, part of his stock in trade. His face was a fiery claret, under the chalky white of his albino eyelashes, the inverted source of his nickname. In their instinctive and terrifying war against life, as presented to them in Moorhill, every means was fair, only a victim — for money or amusement, or both — necessary. Although they did not say much, sinking their noses luxuriously into their stout glasses, they registered with disapproval John's insistence.

'What do you mean, Rooney? Aren't we among friends?'

'That's right,' said Andy Cleggan graciously. 'Willy Boyle was always a decent man. I always said that. Isn't that right, boys?'

'Right. Willy Boyle is the heart of corn.'

Leaning on the counter, the barman watched them with growing distaste. He had planned to leave for half an hour or so about this time, to catch a meal, and, more important, to

feed his greyhound which was probably slavering for its bit of
steak. But he was troubled by the rancour in the air, the obscure quarrelsomeness of Willy: if anything happened, his
mother wouldn't be able to handle it. A fair was good for
trade, but countrymen were hard to get rid of: unused to drink,
they lay around all evening gabbing, the porter going sour in
their bellies. And that crew Willy Boyle was playing Pied
Piper to, they could drink an iron lung apiece, but they were
also damned dangerous. If only one could find a way of selling
drink without having to put up with the kind of people
that bought it: they would never tolerate goings-on like that in
Belfast.

Willy Boyle solved his problem for him. At intervals during the afternoon, he had suddenly remembered his enamel
bucket and searched for it frantically, accusing everyone until
it was found. Looking for a reason to reassert himself, the
bucket came to his mind once more, and he began to look for
it wildly. 'Where in hell's that bucket? If any of those Castleisland whures . . .' His attendants searched for it with assiduous
servility and discovered it sitting on a case of empties near the
entrance to the kitchen. Andy Cleggan passed it to him, rever-
ently. Enraged by such promptness, Willy let it fall slapbang
on the floor.

'Are you calling calves, Willy?' said one man in the corner,
civilly. He was a fair-haired Presbyterian, called George
Booth, with the rather attractive slow smile of someone at ease
with himself and the world.

'It's good I have them to call anyway, and don't plan to
buy other people's,' snarled Willy. This was meant to be a hit
at Booth who had sold one of his farms and was rumoured to
be moving into town to set up as a dealer. Since the Booths
had been strong farmers in the Castleisland district since

Plantation times the move was regarded, on both sides, as a failure to maintain tradition.

'Mind your tongue, there,' warned Tom Jackson, 'or there's some as will mind it for you.'

Willy laid down his glass slowly and, teetering back towards the wall, squared himself into what he considered a fighting position, left hand thrust forward, right poised behind his head in menace. John Rooney hovered around him like a distracted mother-hen.

'I won't take lip from any dirty get of a Protestant, anyway,' said Willy, glaring at the other end of the bar.

In the commotion that followed, everyone participated, in hot confusion. Booth, Jackson and the others rose from their seats and plunged vaguely towards Willy to be halted by the imploring gestures of John Rooney: 'Never mind him, now, he's drunk and he doesn't mean a word of it.'

'Maybe you'd like a touch yourself,' said Tom Jackson, brandishing a knobbly fist.

Behind John Rooney, Andy Cleggan and his associates formed a wavering second line of defence: 'Easy on, now men, easy on.' In the background Willy Boyle danced in dervish rage, daring all to come. The two groups swayed back and forwards, voices heavy with drink, until, whipping off his apron, the barman came around hurriedly to separate them.

'Come on, now, Willy,' he said, pointedly, 'you'll have to go. There's no room for that kind of chat here.'

'What chat?' said Willy, sullenly. 'It was them started it.'

'You'll have to go now, Willy, and that's flat,' said the barman, with the double authority of a sober man and a property holder on whose premises a misdemeanour has been committed. 'I won't stand for that class of mischief making.' He grasped Willy by the collar.

'Come on, Willy,' said John Rooney, seeing his chance.

'That's right,' said Andy Cleggan, with lofty decision, 'come on, Willy, we will not stay where we are not wanted.'

His companions agreed, with pleasing unanimity that they would not stay where any one of their number was not wanted.

Mollified, Willy led his troop towards the door, with the air of a betrayed but undefeated general. 'It'll be a long time,' he said bitterly, with his head still inside, 'before I darken this door again.'

'Good riddance,' said the barman, as the door banged behind them.

In the middle of Main Street, the group assembled in glum silence. It was twilight now, and the lights from shop-windows and doors threw butter-yellow rectangles on the pavement. Outside the garageman's concrete of the town cinema a queue was forming, country lads in belted overcoats, shuffling large feet. The drink sour in his stomach, his head throbbing in the cool air, John Rooney reflected sadly that it was the first time he had ever been thrown out of a pub: The Mountain Rest into the bargain. If his father heard of it, he would kick up holy murder: he had always given his patronage to The Mountain Rest and regarded it as a 'good country pub'. Maybe he should wait a while, until he sobered up, before going home. The busy millrace of the normal life of the street made him realise how far gone he was: he swayed slightly on his feet.

'What'll we do now?' said Willy Boyle, doubtfully.

There was a pause and then Andy Cleggan cleared his throat.

'What about going down to the Glory Hole for a wee sup before we go?' he said, with anxious heartiness.

'They mightn't let us in,' said Willy Boyle. A policeman passed, pushing a bicycle, his cape black as a bat, his Sten-gun gleaming. He looked curiously at the group in the middle of the street. 'They mightn't let us in when we have drink taken elsewhere. It's getting late, you know.'

'Yer all right,' said Dandy MacHugh. 'There's no keeping out or putting out down there. You'll be welcome.'

'Better not,' said John Rooney, in half-hearted protest.

'Come on,' said Willy, decisively.

The Glory Hole, otherwise known as the Dead End, was the most notorious pub in Moorhill, spoken of by the matrons of the town as though it were an antechamber of hell. It belonged to a bachelor called 'Sheriff' MacNab, who, though he lived over the pub, had never been known to drink himself, preferring poker and 'the nags'. Formerly a coachhouse, it had, as the saying goes, seen better days, but its gaunt façade, distempered a bilious yellow, was still impressive. It stood directly in front of the old Protestant graveyard; emerging on a moonlit night to relieve a full bladder, one was confronted by ranks of tombstones on the hill opposite: an accusing army of puritan dead. It was reputed for its bad drink, served at all hours of the day and night, despite the vigilance of the Royal Ulster Constabulary. It was even more reputed for the curious things that happened there, especially to strangers who fell into the cunning hands of its clientele. A commercial traveller from Enniskillen, a dignified, moustachioed gentleman of the old school, had woken to find himself stark naked in the town river. A hard-boiled sergeant of the WAAF's had found her underwear flying from the top of the War Memorial. It was the operational headquarters of Andy Cleggan and his friends, who, when God was good, ended the night in a drunken stupor in one of the straw-filled outhouses. Its real name, executed in straggly Gothic letters over the door, was the Moorhill Arms, and it was, in its way, the most lively place in Moorhill.

As they trooped into the low-ceilinged room, John Rooney trailing behind, they were greeted enthusiastically. The thin middle-aged man behind the bar raised his palm in a salute, Indian-style.

'Well, if it isn't Long Willy Boyle, the terror of the prairies, and his side-kick Big John Rooney, the fastest plough alive. Howdy, partners. Tie your horses to the hitching-post and name your poison!'

Willy Boyle blinked. He was suspicious and a little awed by the fluency of the greeting; but it seemed friendly, particularly after his ejection from The Mountain Rest. He felt suddenly generous.

'Whiskey for all,' he declared.

'Better stick to the stout,' advised John Rooney.

'Firewater for five,' said the man behind the bar, reaching for a bottle of MacDimnocks Special Scotch Whiskey and measuring out five halves swiftly, below counter level. 'And how is life in the prairie these days? Any Indians? Any Sioux smoke-signals betokening death to the white man?' He pushed a glass across to Willy. 'Any Blackfeet squaws?'

'Damn the one,' said Willy fervently. MacNab was obviously a wee bit touched, but he was a friendly man, unlike some he could name. And he wasn't too far wrong about the women.

'Spoken like a true cowboy. A man's best friend is his horse. Isn't that right, Andy?'

'Willy Boyle,' said Andy Cleggan, heavily, 'is no common cowpoke. He is the best rancher south of the Sperrins. He drove a herd to town today the like of which was never seen on the old Chisholm Trail, let alone the wide ranges of Black Mountain and Castleisland.'

'They were damned good cattle, all right,' agreed Willy happily. 'And I made a damned good deal. Another round there, men.'

Three hours later Willy Boyle was explaining, for the tenth time, to a large and steadily growing audience, first, how he had triumphed in his bargain and then, how he had given the Castleisland men their comeuppance. His speech was nearly as incomprehensible as that of Black Barney: he left sentences trailing in mid-air, ran words wildly into each other; sometimes, he would stand for a moment or two in baffled silence, as though he had lost something, peering intently down the well of his consciousness. Finding nothing, but painfully aware of some lack of coherence, he would cover the transition with oaths and imprecations.

'I showed them, the bastards, I showed them, didn't I, damn them?'

'You did indeed,' said Andy Cleggan, draping an enormous arm over his tiny shoulders, and belching warmly. 'You're a murderous man when you start, Willy Boyle. We were all afraid of what you might take into your head to do.'

'I wouldn't like to face you, Long Willy,' said 'Gentleman' Jim Brady, winking at the audience. The 'Gentleman', Andy Cleggan's closest crony, was a local strong man, famous for his double-jointed fists, which, for the price of a drink, he could make crack like pistol-shots. Although never properly trained, he had fought briefly as an amateur with the local Don Bosco club, smothering the majority of his opponents by the unprincipled violence of his attacks, until a more experienced referee had spotted his repertoire of rabbit and kidney punches.

'He'd be dangerous, all right,' everyone agreed, admiringly. Everyone, that is, except Jimmy the Jail, who had achieved the oblivion he sought, his grizzled poll sunk on a barrel-head, and John Rooney who sat beside him, in a waking doze, his eyes glazed, his body slumping forward every now and then, like a badly filled sack.

'But a generous man withal,' said Andy, raising what Sheriff MacNab called his sombrero, with a fine gesture. 'No kindlier friend.'

'Generish,' agreed Black Barney, his red shirt open to the navel, his eyes wild under his tattered black hat.

'No truer friend,' said Dandy MacHugh.

Puzzled but pleased, Willy made a gallant attempt to acknowledge this recognition of his merits. 'All friends here,' he said, and then paused. 'Set them up again, Sheriff.' He rummaged in his pockets and produced a diminished bundle of notes which he placed on the counter. 'All friends here,' he muttered briefly again, and then closed his eyes, and shuddered, as another bout of nausea passed swiftly over him, like a large green wave over a very small boat.

Whose idea the football match was would be hard to say. It was an hour after closing time and they were still drinking behind closed shutters, by the light of a candle behind the bar and the minute glow of a red Sacred heart lamp from the kitchen. It was probably big Andy, who had reached the stage where he showed everyone the medal he had received as a minor footballer, twenty years ago. As he held the tiny silver-plated disc aloft, his eyes became moist with fond memory. 'I was ten stone then, and as fit as a fiddle,' he said sadly, as though speaking of the dead. Or it may have been Gentleman Jim, who had been describing a game the previous Sunday, between Moorhill Gaels and Fentown Pearses. In his eagerness to demonstrate the winning goal, he had taken Black Barney's hat (the head it covered had long lost any sense, not merely of ownership, but of reality), rolled and tied it into a ball, and placed it carefully on the floor in front of him. With a neat swipe of the instep, the professional's penalty kick, he sent it flying past Andy Cleggan. 'Up Moorhill!' he roared. 'Offside!' trumpeted Big Andy, confusing his codes.

Befuddled but eager, the drinkers plunged into the fray. At first, there was the semblance of sides. Willy Boyle was appointed captain of the Fentown team, but since he had been sick only an hour before, the position was titular. Gentleman Jim was, therefore, Acting Captain, Andy Cleggan opposing him; the goalposts were stout bottles. But in the poorly lit pub, the small black hat was almost indistinguishable; body crashed into body in confusion. Placing his head well down, Andy Cleggan ploughed through the room like a rogue elephant. 'Moorhill abu!' he roared, but as he poised for a kick at goal he found that the hat had disappeared, and only a piece of white string remained.

After a brief moment it was found, wedged under a door, and disintegrated into flitters. 'We need something easier to see,' said Andy, with keen disappointment. Referee Dandy MacHugh, resourceful and dapper, appeared carrying a large white object and placed it down before Andy. 'There you are,' he said, 'a new Croke Park pigskin.' Andy drew back his boot and sent the enamel bucket sailing through the air to land with a smack in the lap of John Rooney. With a start, Rooney awoke, and shot to his feet, sending the bucket clanging to the floor again.

The effect produced by the bucket, the kick and fall following each other in the darkened room like claps of thunder, was instantaneous. James MacNab shot from behind the bar into the centre of the group: 'Now men, you'll have to go. Fun's fun, but a noise like that will bring the police down on us, like a ton of bricks.' Willy Boyle, who was dully aware that there was something wrong and resented the sudden shift of attention from himself that the football match had produced, suddenly recognised his bucket, 'Jesus,' he said, with a squeal of rage, 'you curse of God whures, you've ruined me good bucket.' He bent down to cradle it in his arms: a shower of enamel drifted to the floor like flakes of snow. Shock, and an empty stomach, combined to produce a sudden, chilled sobriety: 'Where are the sponging bastards?' he said, bitterly, looking around the room. Andy Cleggan, Gentleman Jim Brady and Dandy MacHugh were nowhere to be seen: neither was John Rooney.

When the bucket had landed in his lap, bringing him sharply awake, John Rooney did not know where he was. The smoke-filled room, the swaying bodies, it was like a nightmare, and for a moment he wondered if he was dead and lost for ever. Then he remembered, shame and pain mounting in his skull and a retching spasm in the stomach, and his first thought was to escape in the night air.

It was raining slightly, a light damp rain that was like a blessing on the drumtap in his temples. A full white moon occupied the sky. He saw the yard stretching down towards the river, the shapes of the bottling shed, the old barn, a heeled up cart like a gallows. He picked his way, gingerly, over the bright stones of the yard to a darkened corner. On the slope opposite, the gravestones of the old Protestant cemetery rode the night like the white sails of sailing ships in a long forgotten school book. Protestants, he reflected as he peed, were a funny class of people: they didn't believe in Purgatory, for example. But then, how did you know what Purgatory was like, anyway? Then, there was this history business: one minute they were Irish, and the next, they were English, whichever suited them. Why couldn't they just forget the past and then, maybe, we could all live together as neighbours, happily ever after. There was no point in stirring up bad blood the way Willy Boyle did; live and let live was what he felt, whoever was wrong, and the more credit if you forgave your oppressor. The calm, perfect night filled him with mild benevolence.

As he was buttoning his trousers he heard, as in a dream, voices behind him, quarrelling voices.

'No point in going back, now.'

'That bloody bucket put the kybosh on it. Why the hell couldn't you leave it alone?'

'Why did you suggest the game, you stupid cur?'

'It wasn't my idea. It was your big brain thought it up.'

'A good night ruined.'

'Who's that galoot standing over there, listening to us?'

'That's that Rooney. If he'd had his way, there would have been no night at all. Yapping for his home all day like a child.'

'Dirty spoilsport. Will I get him?'

'No bloody harm.'

As the first blow struck him, sharply, in the back of the neck, below the ear, John Rooney turned, astonishment and shock lengthening his features. 'We're all friends, here, men,' he said, with obscure conviction. The next blow caught him full on the mouth and he staggered backwards. Just as he was wondering what to say or do, all the gravestones in the Protestant cemetery began to topple in on him, avengingly.

Willy Boyle poised for a last diatribe at the back door of the pub. 'Easy now, Willy,' said James MacNab, 'or you'll bring the police down on top of us.'

'Right good lesson for you if I did,' shrilled Willy. 'And the rest of that pack too. Not a dacent man among them.' And then, a thought striking him, 'Where's John Rooney?'

'He went home,' said a voice from the shadows, behind the publican's shoulder.

'He did not,' said Willy vehemently. 'John Rooney would never leave a man the way you would.'

'Maybe he'll come back in a minute or two. Hold your horses and we'll have a quiet drink and wait for him.'

'He's hereabouts somewhere,' said Willy Boyle, 'and wherever hell he is, I'll find him. I won't leave this town the night without him.'

A search party, led (reluctantly) by MacNab and (militantly) by Willy, probed the length of the yard. In the bottling shed, stumbling over a forest of empty bottles, they heard something moving and flashed a match on it. It was a mouse, which regarded them for a moment with beady, unfrightened eyes, and then scuttled away. Knee-deep in moonlight, figures swayed drunkenly, like bathers in a long stretch of surf, poking in the nettle-wild remains of a coachshed, examining with a desperate summoning of interest a sagging clothes-line, a discarded outdoor wooden closet. But it was Willy Boyle who finally found John Rooney where he had been thrown, at the base of the triangle of the uptilted cart. His face was badly cut, with a gash across the forehead. As Willy, calling for help, knelt at his side, his left eye opened, and he regarded Willy briefly, then spat out a particle of tooth and a dark gobbet of blood.

'I meant no harm,' he muttered thickly.

'Of course you didn't,' said Willy, in deep misery.

James MacNab came hurrying down the yard, carrying a bucket of water in one hand, and a sponge in the other: he passed them both to Willy. As the enamel flashed, milkwhite in the pale clarity of the moonlight, a thought seemed to stir in John Rooney's mind, like a fish turning in deep water.

'Did you get your bucket, Willy,' he whispered through broken lips.

Willy held the bucket out, at arm's length. There was evidently a small hole in the side, for a thin stream of water trickled onto their clothes.

'The only clean thing in this town,' he said, with defiant bitterness. Then he began to swab away the blood from his friend's face. His hands were still awkward, and he fumbled.

'Up Moorhill,' said John Rooney, wincing as the sponge touched his eye.

'Up Moorhill,' agreed Willy Boyle, bleakly.

The Oklahoma Kid

IT WAS my Cowboy period. On the fringe of the newly ploughed field behind our house I practised my draw, with two sticks peeled and whittled to revolver shape. There was the simple hip draw, like Buck Jones, thumbs resting on the belt, fingers crisply spread, like eagle's talons. Then as your opponent moved (batted an eye nervously, before slapping leather), the releasing plunge downward to action. A double explosion — Bang, Bang! — and a thistle fell dead, in the full pride of its pale, prickly life. The daisies shook their sunbonnet heads in dismay while all the other thistles moved (despite their roots) a step backwards: the Oklahoma Kid was in charge.

Then there was the border cross draw, hands flat across the stomach, relaxed but dangerous as serpents. A cow moved its flank to shudder off a fly and the serpents uncoiled. Twin mouths of flame flickered in the air, gun-smoke and cordite (I did not know they were irreconcilable) drifting across the spring grass.

Tim, our farm horse, watched me, a green scum of grass on his protruding lower lip and wedge-shaped teeth. I renamed him Thunder and rode to town, his flanks glistening with sweat, his glove-deep nostrils pulsing as he heaved for breath. Unconcerned, he lashed his tail, dropped his head to lip in a daisy, and I saw the harness marks on his neck, the sagging belly roped with veins, and felt oddly ashamed. A smell of clover, the drone of a bee away into silence, and the prairies of my imagination — long grass of Wyoming, red-rock mesa of Arizona — dwindled to a boy in dungarees standing in a field in County Tyrone; Northern Ireland to some, Ulster to others.

Hearing my aunt call I raced in, tamely: someone was looking for me in the shop.

Every day, the country people came down the mountain roads to our house. Some came punctually to collect their pensions, for it was a sub-Post Office, and one of my aunts was postmistress. White-haired, gaunt as a rake, she stood in her little office among the weighing scales and postal regulations, indicating where X his or her mark should go. Others came to buy odds and ends, liquorice allsorts, Paris buns, MacLean's Headache Powders from what had been, in my grandfather's time, a flourishing shop and to which they were still attached by strands of loyalty. One family came — one or other of seven identical children, lugging a basket as big as himself across the fields – because they had quarrelled with the new grocer, an entirely new and more up-to-date business, half a mile down the road.

These were the usual callers, bound by no regulations (though the post-office was supposed to close at 3 p.m.) except weather and the rhythm of work on the land. A dry day in winter, a wet in summer presented equal opportunities but, generally, they preferred to come at twilight, thus saving labour and light. Which is why I remember the shop as a scene by La Tour, the people standing well back in the shadows, my aunt's white head bent close to a grease-spattered candle, a smell of damp clothes, bread, cream of tartar, pervasive as the smell of paint in a studio. They loved her, unjudging audience of all their troubles, but they wore her out.

During the winter, we had another group of callers: those who came to borrow books. For our house was also a branch of the Tyrone County (Carnegie) Library and my other aunt was Honorary Librarian. As she was often occupied around the farm, I was consulted as Deputy Librarian. Already, at ten, I was a formidable bookworm, imagination sprouting in isolation like one of those sickly potato stalks one finds in cellars. A hundred books came each quarter, arranged in wooden cases with hasps like pirate trunks. Sixty fiction, twenty juvenile and twenty general knowledge and by the end of a month I would be familiar with the contents of some and the titles of all, and be able to advise with authority. Ranged on the half-empty shelves, they soon smelt like all the other commodities, faintly sweet and musty, with patterns of damp on the bindings.

The main demand was for fiction. At school, few of the older children read, plunging directly into the work of the farm when they came home. So the Juveniles lay unused except for my predatory dismissal. And General Knowledge meant little to the people of the district, speculative only about local things. Even books on farming, with their background of hops, cider and Harvest Festivals seemed far removed from life on the soggy hillfarms of Tyrone. So it was fiction they sought, to fill the long hours of the winter nights. And fiction consisted of only two kinds, Love Stories and Cowboys.

The Love Stories were my aunt's domain. A reader herself, she sampled them before passing them on, and not only for pleasure. Many of the farmers' wives read, but the most voracious were two large ladies, one seventy and one fifty, one single and one married, alike only in their unslakeable thirst for that mysterious thing called Romance. If my aunt was out, she would have left a selection aside, which I would pass over the counter, primed for the moral discussion which seemed inextricable from Love Stories.

'Is there any Love in it?' they asked, peering at the title doubtfully in the poor light. Ruby M. Ayres, Isobel C. Clarke, Annie S. Swan, Ethel M. Dell — how I remember those romantic sounding names! And the titles, *A Stranger to Paradise*, *The Primrose Path*, *An Open Heart*, wicket gates to a world where slender, flowering English girls called Penelope or Millicent awaited the dreamlike destiny of love. No one found it strange that, like the books on farming, they should always deal with settings completely foreign to us: books were like that, a province of the unreal.

'Your aunt said the last was good, but there was damn all love in it.'

'There's plenty this time,' I said, hedging furiously.

'Is it good love or the other sort?'

'The other sort', that vice to which love-stories were prone, was beyond me, but I could parrot a testimony. With childish cunning I saw that what they deplored, they secretly coveted: the question was a necessary moral front.

'It's mostly good,' I said, 'but there's a doubtful bit at the end.'

When the choice came to be made, however, the questionable book generally went into the basket, joining the Inglis Pan loaf, the pot of Richhill Jam, the Andrew's Liver Salts. I had no illusions about love stories: in any case, I was delighted to be accepted in complicity in an adult mystery. But my capacity to corrupt was limited: the really questionable books, the ones entirely devoted to love of the wrong sort, had already been locked away by my far-seeing aunt.

With the Cowboy stories I came into my own. I had only recently graduated from Juveniles (the face of the prince suddenly shaded by a sombrero, the witch changing her broomstick for a rustler's pinto) and for a time the charm of mere killing was enough. But I was in search of more than the elementary violence of the Wild West Club, and when I discovered my first Zane Grey, I knew I was in for a long ride. It was *Riders of the Purple Sage*, and when the boulder rolled down, sealing off the Mormon family in the valley, I quivered with excitement. I asked Mr Ferguson the post van driver, who spent the day in a little hut at the end of our turfshed (it was the end of his thirty-mile run) before driving back in the afternoon to head-office, whether Zane Grey had written many books. He said that he had seen in the paper once that Zane Grey was a woman and that she had written over a hundred books, many of them posthumous. This information puzzled but pleased me: a hundred books would take a long time to read.

I can see now that the hallucinatory hold these stories gained on me was because I connected them with a mysterious previous life. Every six months or so, Mr Ferguson brought long blue envelopes bearing flamboyant stamps to remind me that I had an existence elsewhere in the mind of a father, who had sent me back, during the Depression, to the only place where he had been happy. How was I to know that Arizona was nearly a continent away from Bushwick Avenue, Brooklyn, where only cigarstore Indians were to be seen, and that in fostering my dream I was cancelling that of my father?

My circle of fellow-readers was small but intense. Besides Mr Ferguson (who hardly qualified since I saw him only on Saturdays when I was free from school), there was a dark-jowled young man called Dan Lynch, who lived with his mother and sister on one of the most remote farms under the shadow of Coal Hill. With his hat crushed on his head, he would swing in onto the gravel before the house and leap from his bicycle as though from a lathered horse. Henry Anderson, on the other hand, was a gaunt Presbyterian farmer who demanded my advice gravely before making his choice. If Dan was the typical hardjawed cowboy, Henry Anderson was the Mormon preacher or sheriff, just, severe, taciturn. When he gave back the book, it was generally wrapped in a page from *The Farmer and Stockbreeder* upon which he had laboriously noted the words he could not understand. Hugh Kelly, who

drove Gormley's lorry around the back lanes made a fourth.
There were others, like John Mooney, our serving man, who
read an occasional book, but these were the cream of the outfit.

To these rather quiet, hard-working men, my childish insistence was at first strange, then amusing. Cowboy stories had
been for them a recreation after a hard day's work, but I demanded more. Before passing out a book I would give a
judgement and expect one in return. If there were too many
people in the house, we talked by the roadside, turning over
pages by the light of a hissing carbide bicycle lamp. The in-
congruity of the scene did not strike us: briefly we shared the
illusion of a wider world, with electric storms crackling over
the prairies, stampeding the wild horses. Was that the sound of
hooves on the Belfast road?

One thing did trouble me, although I was afraid to speak of
it. We were all agreed that Zane Grey was the best. Although
Clarence Mulford and W.C. Tuttle were also good, they
lacked the authentic detail of *Wildfire* and *West of the Pecos*.
But there was such a lot about women in some of Zane Grey
(perhaps he was one after all?) who were often discovered
without their denim shirts, a warm flush mantling neck and
bosom. This was all right if the hero was involved, because he
had the shyness of chivalry, but when, in one story, a vicious
outlaw kept a woman chained in a cave, I was dismayed: the
Cowboy stories seemed to be following the Love stories. That
the scene filled me with a new feeling, at once hot and guilty,
dismayed me even more: was I turning outlaw? I finally
showed the book to my aunt who took a brief glance at it and
put it away, without comment. But what was so fascinating
about naked women? Whipping my imaginary mustang as I
drove the cows home from the hill pastures in the evening, I
wished I knew the answer.

My great sadness, however, was that, as the winter ended, the work of the fields slowly reclaimed my cowboy friends. First it was the ploughing. Coming home from school, I would see another field opened and wave to a figure on a headland, turning with his team. Then, as the days lengthened, there was the sowing; when the oats were in, I would be staying at home a few days to help with the cutting and planting of the seed potatoes. In the meantime, people read still, but more slowly, taking as much as a month to finish a book. Soon they would stop reading altogether.

It was then that I heard about the film. Someone had seen in the local market town a poster announcing the coming of *The Greatest Cowboy Film of All Time — The Oklahoma Kid*. I had been to a few films (each year a visiting priest showed slides of Mission work on a sheet in the local hall) but this was different, and not to be missed. After dinner, I ran out to bring the news to my fellow-readers where they were working in the fields. Henry Anderson was gathering dried potato stalks and burning them by the riverside.

'What do you think we should do?' I asked.

He threw another gripful of stalks on the pyre, which fumed a grey-black smoke.

'I'll have to talk to the others,' he said, slowly. 'But if it is as good as you say, I think we should go.'

Several nights later, at the end of the week, we met at the crossroads to discuss the situation. Henry, as the eldest, led the conversation, proposing that we should club together and hire Gormley's Hackney.

'How much would that be?' asked Dan Lynch anxiously.

'Gormley generally charges two quid for the run, but he'd give it to me for less,' said Hugh, with an expert's smooth knowledge. 'Not counting the cub here, that makes about ten shilling a skull.'

Although the sum was far beyond my savings, I was decided not to relinquish my equality.

'I'll pay for myself,' I said, with defiance.

'If the nadger pays that makes a four-way split; are you
game?'

We all looked at Dan. Despite his habitual cheerfulness,
everyone knew that he found it a hard struggle to support his
mother and sister on the tiny farm and that he rarely had
pocket money, even for cigarettes. Nevertheless we could not
offer him a loan, however well meant, because it would indicate that we knew his plight, and reticence in money matters
was one of the facts of the countryside.

'If you can find a fifth man,' Dan said finally, 'I'm game.'

For the following week, we talked of little or nothing but
the film. According to Hugh Kelly, the principal part was
taken by an actor who had been a cowboy himself, and the
whole thing would be authentic, down to the last cowclap.
Even the taciturnity of Henry Anderson dissolved before such
golden possibilities: 'It might be a real good night,' he said.
As for myself, I rehearsed the scene daily after school in the
fields behind the house. It would be the first time I had ever
gone to town, on my own account, without a watchful relative.

It was not until the evening we left that I learned who was
to be the extra man. They had canvassed several people, including casual readers like John Mooney, but all said they had
neither money nor time for such a foolish jaunt at a busy time
of year. There was one man in the parish, however, who was
well known never to refuse the chance of an outing, however
long or for whatever purpose. In despair, therefore, they asked
Papa (short for Peter Anthony) Cummins.

Papa was a smallish, rather dusty-looking man, who always sported a green hat with a large chicken feather stuck
under the band; together with his mottled complexion, it made
him look an ageing Indian brave. This, however, was the only

relevant thing about him, from our point of view, because he openly scorned books, all the more so since his wife was one of the two Romance addicts. His chosen activities were card-playing — he was a deadly hand at twenty-five, the favourite game in the district — and above all, talking. From morning till night his flow of chatter went on, ceaseless and indiscriminate as a river, down which floated anything, dead dogs, cornstalks, old turds. Seeing him approach, people doubled on their tracks, disappeared under bridges, vanished in a cloud of pipesmoke, but he was still there when they reappeared, a bucket or spade tucked jauntily under his arm, his nasal voice grinding away at their wits.

My own uneasiness where Papa was concerned was simple: his outspokenness troubled me. Generally, country people never talked much about themselves. But Papa recognised none of this reticence, speaking of his wife, for instance, as casually as though she were something he had picked up at the Hiring Fair. His conversation was spiked with jokes and innuendoes, which by the subdued guffaws that greeted them, I guessed to be somehow connected with the Love stories. My prudish altar-boy's soul was both fascinated and revolted.

But there was a further reason. As I grew older, the strangeness of my situation troubled me increasingly: not only could I scarcely remember my life in America, but I could hardly even remember my father. With the indifference of the hardworked, my aunts did not speak much of the past and failed to understand my secret pleas for information. My main hope lay then in what casual knowledge I could find. Patient as an archaeologist, I reconstituted the past from old books and photographs and the rambling conversation of the older men in the parish. The image of my father I got was vague but flattering, that of a red-haired young man who sang occasionally at dances and was a demon for practical jokes. Only Papa among the men of my father's generation refused to answer my questions and I sensed he disapproved. Once when someone, in the way of adults, placed his hand on my head and asked what I was going to be when I grew up, he rounded sharply, before I could speak, and said with a rough emphasis I have never forgotten:

'He'll probably be a blackguard, like his father before him.'

At the crossroads, that evening, Papa was the first to arrive. Typically enough, he had not changed, his hands stuck in the pockets of his overalls, a newly cut ashplant under one armpit. The others had washed after coming in from the fields, their faces shone a scrubbed red and they had on soft Sunday shoes. When Hugh appeared with the car, his arm dangling self-consciously through the driver's window, the group was complete. It was a big Vauxhall and we all piled in, Papa in front and the three of us in the back.

The whole journey was dominated by the whine of Papa's voice. Henry and Dan sat on either side of me, their hands square on their knees. It had been a damp day and the landscape had that stereoscopic brightness that sometimes comes after rain, or just before twilight. On either side, men were still working in the fields. My companions should have been delighted with this chance to observe the methods and progress of others, but they seemed striken with self-consciousness. Only Papa kept his eyes open, delivering a running commentary as we passed: 'That's good even ploughing now,' or, 'The man drove that furrow should be shot.'

Outside Strulebridge, where the river curled under a grey bridge, there was one field sloping directly into the sun, in which the green shoots of an early crop were just beginning to appear. A sight like this was so rare that I expected a comment, but all my companions did, when Papa drew their attention to it, was to knead their caps slowly, nodding assent to his admiring; 'There's a right snappy farmer for you!' What was wrong with them, and why were things not going as I had expected?

Soon we were at the outskirts of the town, the wealthy well-tended grounds of large private houses, the golf-course with its striding pylons. Strulebridge, a sturdy market centre with about eight thousand population, was ten miles or so from my home. I was brought to it twice or three times a year on shopping expeditions, and its main street, dominated by the Courthouse and the War Memorial, was my only real image of urban life, contrasting with my half-memories of America. As we turned in the Belfast road, I felt a familiar excitement, all the sharper because I was now entering for the first time as an equal among adults. There was the long low shape of the County Library, the centre room which all our books came. Above it appeared the twin-spired silhouette of the Diocesan Cathedral, with the college in its shadow to which I might be going in a year or two. All these details seemed to fuse into a mysterious and seductive whole, promising something subtly different from the pace of the farm. My awareness of Papa's presence diminished: the Oklahoma Kid was finally coming to town.

There was further dimension to this new and potent image: the town was nervous with change. This was wartime, and through Main Street paraded a detachment of British soldiers. We stopped the car at the foot of the courthouse to let them pass. First came a tall man wearing a busby and leopard skin, his eyes fixed fiercely ahead, runnels of sweat coursing down his jaw. Then drummers, left legs dragging with the weight of their instruments, upon which they gave an occasional marching pace rattle. Then pipers, in kilt and cloak, with white mouth-pieces resting on their shoulders. Behind was the rank and file, in sober khaki, polished boots clattering, arms rising and falling like puppets. Under the sand-bagged court-

house they marched, out the Barracks Road, and in the distance we heard the band strike up again at the drum-major's
harsh command. Its sudden flourish shot a shiver down my
spine.

We were not the only ones to have stopped to watch. Along
the pavement was a thin line of people, still in attitudes of listening. Some seemed countrymen, like ourselves, their inex-
perience betrayed by their weighty pose. A few customers had
emerged from shops, packages in hand; there were even one or
two shopkeepers, wearing their white aprons. But most of the
onlookers were girls, of every shape, size and age, their eyes
bright, their lips wounded with lipstick.

'There's no shortage of women about here,' said Papa, ap-
preciatively, looking around him.

In order to be in time for the film, we had agreed that it
was better not to eat at home but to have something in town.
After a hurried fish-and-chips in Danielli's, we made our way
towards the cinema — it was the smallest of the three in town
— which lay through a maze of sidestreets. Our pace was
slow, because the pavements were clogged with people. At
first, we took for granted that they were shoppers, but, as we
elbowed our way in single file, it gradually dawned on us that
they were mainly soldiers. Of various ranks and regiments
(thick serge of the Inniskillings, black berets of the tank corps,
light blue of the RAF), they pushed their way along, obviously
at ease and at home. And when we finally got to the cinema,
we found them again, a large queue of fighting men and their
girls, stretching straight down the street and round the corner.
Five sheepish Oklahoma Kids come to a twentieth-century
town, we stood looking on: there was not the remotest hope of
getting in.

It was as we were making our way despondently back to
the car that Hugh suggested that perhaps we would have a

chance of getting into the new cinema. This magnificent building, a concrete palace called the Coliseum, stood right in the centre of Main Street, between Littlewood's and Woolworth's. Ordinarily, it would never have occurred to us to try such a place, which had the reputation of being very expensive, and was frequented mainly by townspeople. There was added reason for suspicion which my companions understood but I did not. Run up by a local contractor to cater to the new trade brought by the war, it was decorated in the Arabian Nights style, with spangles and stars on the ceiling and double love-seats at the back. These latter had brought down the wrath of Canon Kerr, the fiery old administrator of St John's, who described them in an Easter sermon as 'hot seats to Hell'.

Now, however, the Coliseum seemed the ideal solution. In the discreet, carpet-heavy hall, a queue was filing, supervised by a splendid commissionaire in sky-blue uniform and cap. It was a long queue, but unlike the tinroofed cinema at the end of town, the atmosphere was orderly and the rate of absorption regular. Fenced by plush ropes we waited, stolid as oxen, whiling away the time by looking at publicity stills or testing the carpets in which, as Papa said, one could sink to the fetlocks. Finally, the commissionaire came over to us:

'Two first,' he said. 'Main film's begun.'

'What's that?' asked Henry anxiously.

'He means we'll have to separate,' Hugh explained.

'I'll take the caddy,' said Papa promptly. 'Where do we go now?'

Bumping through the darkness after the cinema attendant's torch, we found ourselves going down the vast shelving floor of the auditorium. Every row seemed filled, a sea of dark heads. Nearer and nearer loomed the screen until the usherette led the way across in front of it. As we followed, I saw a tiny box-shaped shadow rising and falling at the bottom of the screen: it was Papa's hat. At the far corner, underneath the double sign EXIT/GENTLEMEN, were two empty places. Seats banged as we sat down. 'They don't give you much room for your legs,' commented Papa, turning himself several times, like a dog, before settling.

Directly above us, high and insubstantial as cloud formation, reared the images of the film. A window opened like a gulf at the back of a modern apartment to reveal a vista of skyscrapers. A man crossed the screen, his legs, distorted by the angle of vision, grasshopper long. He was speaking angrily to a woman whose face suddenly swam up to us in close-up: beautiful, sad and as huge as a barn door.

'God,' said Papa, 'that's the living spit of young Barney Owen's wife. But I didn't know she wore make-up.'

In a street now, a yellow taxi speeding through the bright lights of the city.

'What's happening?' demanded Papa impatiently, rapping his ashplant against my legs. 'Where are we going?'

It was only then that the truth homed on me. Despite his travelling, Papa had never been to the cinema. His journeys were in search of new listeners, not new sights, and once set down, he continued talking. I remembered with sudden horror a story of how he had gone with a party to the All-Ireland in Dublin and spent the day in a relative's house in Clontarf, listening to the game on the radio. This was the first time he had ever been in a picture house, the first time, indeed, he had ever been affronted by the idea of fiction. What he thought was happening on the screen, whether he regarded these images as real people or shadows, I could not say, since he struck straight through it to whatever everyday life he could recognise.

A man came hurrying down to greet the couple and bring them back through the stage-door.

'That fellow had a wee look of Micky Boyle about the eyes,' Papa announced.

'S-sh,' came from behind us, the first indication that we had an audience.

Inside the theatre, some kind of rehearsal was in progress. Stage-hands were moving in the shadows, shifting scenery, focusing lights. Standing with the couple in the wings, we saw the soprano spotlighted on the stage, her throat distended with sound, her bosoms rising and falling.

'She has the right big udder,' said Papa admiringly.

The comment behind us had risen to an uproar. 'Disgusting,' I heard several times as I tried to sink lower in my seat.

As the singer spread her arms in one final throbbing note, a chorus came tumbling out into the stage, drum majorettes wearing cartwheel cowboy hats and boots, and kicking their long white legs in the air. Papa leaned forward so as to inspect them more closely.

'Where did you say we were?' he asked.

'In New York — in America,' I said, my face flaming.

'By Jasus, they don't wear much in your country. Bare legs and big diddies!'

It was this remark, delivered at the top of his voice, which finally provoked an intervention. From the row behind a soldier thrust his closely cropped head between us.

'Look 'ere, Grandad,' he said mildly, 'you're not the only one in this dump.'

For the first time, Papa became aware of his audience, but without understanding how he had gathered it.

'What the hell's wrong with you?' he said sharply to the head which had landed so unexpectedly in his lap.

'Put a cork in it, will you please,' said the soldier with patient exasperation. And then, seeing that Papa still did not understand: 'Would you mind closing up?'

'Shut up yourself,' said Papa angrily, 'or I'll give you a belt.'

He raised his ashplant in the air: wavy as a spider it appeared on the screen, right across the face of the leading man.

That did it. Cries of protest came from every part of the house, including the balcony. Several people rose in their seats, craning to see what was happening, while the commissionaire raced down the aisle, shining his torch directly into Papa's face.

'I'm afraid you'll have to leave, sir, you're creating a disturbance.'

'What hell disturbance do you mean?' said Papa, 'I'm danged comfortable. And the wee fellow's great: he's explaining it all to me.'

'People are complaining.'

'That's right,' said a hard voice. 'Put him out.'

'Come on,' I said, tugging at Papa's coat. 'We'd better leave.' But I don't think he would have gone except that our three companions suddenly appeared beside us, having heard the row from the other side of the hall.

'I think we'd better go,' said Henry Anderson, gravely.

Everyone turned to watch as we marched out, Papa in front, escorted by the commissionaire, myself last, thankful for the darkness which hid my face. At the door the manager was waiting, a plump little man who hovered around us in dismay.

'There's never been anything like this here before. But we'll refund you your money if you insist.'

But Papa had understood finally and was disgusted.

'You can shove your auld cinema up your ass,' he said sharply, and jamming his hat down on his head, led us out onto the pavement.

I remember one more thing about that evening in Strulebridge. As we passed glumly down the street, a group of boys were standing outside the sliding door of Lyons garage. Several of them wore boiler suits. They watched us with interest and before we were out of earshot, one of them gave a low incredulous whistle.

'That's a right crowd of country-looking idiots,' he said. I looked at my companions. If they had heard him, they did not betray it by the flicker of an eye. Dark-faced and silent, they plunged down the street towards the car.

By right, the story ends there, and anything further will only spoil it. During the return journey, Papa sat at the back and Henry in the front. I don't know what they talked of, or indeed, whether they talked at all, because I soon fell asleep with my head sideways in Papa's lap, from which I had to be lifted when I got home.

But life often adds a postscript; seventeen years later, I descended from a Greyhound Bus in Oklahoma City. In the glaring cafeteria, the voice of Elvis Presley was wolfing through 'Heartbreak Hotel'. Gene Fullmer had just beaten Robinson; the paper I had bought in Salt Lake City the previous night was full of it, since Fullmer was a local man. Eating a sour mess of beef and hash, I began a conversation with the man beside me. He seemed rather disreputable, his hat jammed on his head, his jaws masticating ceaselessly. Yet he also seemed somehow familiar — that great nose, that coppery tint (noticeable under a day-old beard), those wise eyes of legend.

'I'm a Cherokee from Tulsa,' he said, with what I took to be both fatalism and pride. 'What part of Oklahoma do you come from?'

'From Oklahoma City,' I said, involuntarily, 'County Tyrone,' and choked with a mixture of joy, shame and ridiculous conceit.

The Cry

FINALLY HE rose to go to bed. His father had shuffled off a few minutes before and his mother was busy preparing a hot-water bottle, moving, frail as a ghost, through the tiny kitchen. Seeing her white hair, the mother-of-pearl rosary beads dangling from her apron pocket, the bunny rabbit slippers, he felt guilt at keeping her up so late. But he came home so seldom now that he was out of the rhythm of the household and tried to do only what pleased them. And sitting with their big Coronation mugs of cocoa, they had drunk in his presence so greedily that he felt compelled to talk and talk. Mostly of things they had never seen: of travelling in Europe, of what it was like to work on a big newspaper, of the great freedom of living in London. This last had troubled his father very much, centuries of republicanism stirring in his blood.

'What do you mean, son, freedom?'

'I mean, Father, nobody interferes with you. What you do is your own business, provided you cause no trouble.'

Seeing the perplexity in his father's face, he tried to explain in local terms. 'Nobody on *The Tocsin*, for instance would dream of asking if you were Catholic or Protestant — at least not the way they do here. If they did ask, it would be because they were genuinely interested.'

'Then can you explain, son, why England had the reputation she has abroad? Didn't she interfere with freedom everywhere she went, from Africa to the North here?'

'That's not the real England, Father; that's the government and the ruling class. The real Englishman is not like that at all, he stands for individual liberty, live and let live. You should hear them in Hyde Park!'

'I must never have met a real Englishman then,' said his father, obstinately. His face had gone brick-red and his nostrils twitched, showing spikes of white hair. With his bald round head and bright eyes he looked like Chad, in the war-time cartoon, peering over a wall, but it was anger, not humorous resignation, he registered.

'Maybe,' said his mother timidly, 'they're all right when they're at home.'

And there the matter rested. His father had always been violently anti-English: he remembered him saying that he would be glad to live on bread and water for the rest of his life if he could see England brought to her knees. And the struggle there had been when he had first announced his intention of trying to break into newspaper work in London! Dublin would have been all right, or America where his father had spent ten years as a cook in a big hotel, before coming home to marry and settle in the little newsagency business. But England! Religious and political prejudice fused to create his father's image of it as the ultimate evil. And something in his father's harshness called out to him: during his adolescence, he had contacted the local branch of the IRA and tried to join. They (rather he, a lean melancholy egg-packer called Sheridan who had the reputation of being a machine-gunner in the force) had told him to report for a meeting, but when the time came, he had funked it, saying that he had to go away.

And so, Peter changed the conversation. He spoke of shows he had seen, the big American musicals, the Bolshoi and Royal Ballets. But his father still seemed restless: once he saw him glance mournfully across at his mother and wondered what he had said wrong. Her eyes glinted with pleasure as he described a Charity (tactfully amended from Command) Performance, with all the stars arriving in their glittering gowns.

'Oh, that must have been lovely,' she said, with placid yearning.

It was only when he was climbing the stairs, that he realised what his father's glance had meant. 'Good night, now, son, and don't forget to say your prayers,' his mother called after him. That was it; because of his visit, they had not said the regular family rosary, waiting for him to remember and suggest it. How could he explain that he had never seen anyone in England say the rosary, except two Irish lads in his first digs in Camden Town, who had embarrassed everyone by kneeling down at their bedside and saying it aloud in Irish. English Catholics did not believe in loading themselves down with inessentials. But if he had begun to explain all that, they would have jumped to the conclusion that he had lost his faith completely. Religion and politics he should try to leave alone for the short time he was home.

The room was on the top floor, that front bedroom in which he had always slept. The top sheet was turned down, with the same inviting neatness, the blue eiderdown was the same, even the yellow chamber pot beneath the bed. Over the fireplace was the familiar picture of Our Lady of Perpetual Succour, an angular Madonna cradling a solemn-faced Child, a slipper dangling from his chubby foot. Opposite it, on the wall over the bed, was a Victorian sampler, worked by his grandmother as a young girl: THERE IS NO FUN LIKE WORK.

It was all so unchanged that it was almost terrifying, like being confronted with the ghost of his younger self. He heard his father moving in the next room, shifting and sighing. Taking off his clothes, Peter knelt down in his pyjamas for a few moments at the bedside; he hoped the old man would hear the murmur and guess what it was. Then he wandered round the room for something to read.

Spurning *The Wolfe Tone Annual* and *With God on the Amazon* on the dressing table, he discovered a soot-stained copy of *The Ulster Nationalist* which had obviously been taken from the grate to make room for the electric fire; this he carried triumphantly to bed.

The editorial spoke with dignified bitterness of the continued discrimination against Catholics in the North of Ireland in jobs and housing. Facts were given and in spite of the tedious familiarity of the subject Peter felt his anger rise at such pointless injustice. He turned the page quickly to the Court Proceedings:

UNITED NATIONS FOR MOORHILL?

Moorhill Court was taken up on Wednesday with a lengthy hearing of a civil summons for alleged abusive language and assault.

Giving evidence, James MacKennie, Craigavon Terrace, said that Miss Phyllis Murphy had thrown a bucket of water over him as he was passing on his bicycle. Cross-examined witness admitted that he had spoken sharply to Miss Murphy but he had not threatened, as she said, 'to do her.' He admitted borrowing 5/- from Miss Murphy 'to cure a headache'. His solicitor, Mr John Kennedy, said that his client was a veteran of the First World War and had a disability pension. It was true he had been in jail several times, but he was very well thought of in the community.

The defendant, Miss Phyllis Murphy, said that James MacKennie was a well known pest, and besides 'he had been coming over dirty talk'. She denied throwing water over him and said he had been making so many 'old faces' that he had driven over the bucket of water. She denied saying she hoped 'that would make him laugh the other side of his Orange face'.

In giving his decision, the RM said it was difficult case to disentangle but he felt both parties were to blame and he therefore bound them over to keep the peace for a year. It was a pity, now that people were trying to outlaw war, to find neighbours disagreeing; maybe he should ask the United Nations to come to Moorhill . . . (laughter in court).

Peter Douglas read on with delighted horror. For the first time since he had returned, he felt at ease; he threw the paper on the floor, and turned contentedly over to sleep. Somewhere downstairs, the cuckoo clock he had brought his mother was sounding.

II

Some time later, he came suddenly awake to a sound of shouting. He listened carefully, but it could not have come from the next room. Perhaps it was his mother; no, it was too strong, a man's voice. It came from down in the street, but not directly underneath; he sat bolt upright in bed and turned his head towards the window. Yes, there it was again, clearer, and he sounded as if he were in pain.

'O, Jesus, sir, O Jesus, it hurts.'

Maybe somebody had been taken ill suddenly and they were carrying him to the ambulance? Or a fire: he remembered the night, years ago, when old Carolan had been carried out of his house by the firemen, screaming like a stuck pig, rags of cloth still smouldering upon his legs. But who was the man in the street talking to, whom was he calling sir?

'O, Jesus, sir, don't touch me again.'

All across the town lights were beginning to come on; the shadowy figure of a woman, wrapped in a dressing-gown, appeared at the window directly opposite; only something unusual could sanction such loose behaviour in Moorhill. Maybe it was a fight? Then, with a cold rush of certainty, Peter Douglas knew what it was: it was someone being beaten up by the police.

'O, God, sir, don't hit me again.'

The voice was high and pleading. Then there was a scuffle of feet and the sound of a blow, a sharp crack, like a stone on wood. Throwing back the bedclothes, Peter ran to the window and craned out his head. At the bottom of the street, he saw a knot of people. One of them was kneeling on the ground, his shape circled by the light of a torch held by one of the bulky cape-clad figures surrounding him. In the windows above, shadows moved, silent, watching.

'Come on to the barracks now and quit your shouting,' said an impatient voice.

'Oh no, sir, I can't, I'm nearly killed. Somebody help me, for God's sake, please.'

Again the voice was abject, but at a muttered order the torch was extinguished and the four figures closed in on the kneeling man. Was no one going to protest, none of those darkly brooding presences? Peter Douglas opened his mouth to shout, but he was forestalled. A door opened behind the men, letting out a shaft of light. He heard a sharp, educated voice:

'What in blazes do you thugs think you are doing? Leave the man alone.'

One of the four policemen turned, switching his torch directly into the face of the speaker.

'Keep your bloody nose out of it, will ye? Do you want to get a touch too?'

He heard further muttering and then a door slammed angrily. The four figures seized their victim, who now hung like a sack between them, and half-walked, half-ran him down the street towards the barracks. There were no further cries, only the drag of boots on the pavement, an occasional groan and (as the barrack door opened and shut behind them) a gathering silence. One by one the lights went out over the town. Peter Douglas was one of the last to leave, his eyes sore (he had left his glasses on the bedside table) from straining after any further movement. As he climbed into bed again, he heard the cuckoo clock, Cuckoo, Cuckoo, Cuckoo.

III

When he came down to breakfast next morning, after a short and troubled sleep, he found his father waiting impatiently for him. Generally, he was in the shop by this time, but it was his mother's voice he heard, dealing with an early customer: 'Yes, Mrs Wilson, nice weather indeed, for the time of year . . .' And it was his father who prepared the meal, cornflakes, tea and toast, bacon sizzling flagrantly in the pan. It was clear he had something on his mind; Peter felt as suspiciously certain as a prisoner who finds his warder suddenly affable.

'You're pretty lively this morning, aren't you?' he said, digging into the cornflakes.

His father did not reply, fussing around the stove with plates and cloths until, triumphantly, he placed a full plate of bacon, eggs and sausages before his son.

'The old man can do it yet,' he said. Then he sat at the end of the table and watched his son eat, slowly, picking at his food.

'They don't seem to have much appetite in England, anyway,' he said, 'whatever else they have.' And then, without further preamble: 'Did you hear what happened last night?'

'I did,' said his son, briefly. 'Did you?'

'I only heard the tail-end of it, but I heard them all talking this morning.'

'What did they say?'

'They said the B-Specials beat up a young man called Ferguson, whom they accused of being in the IRA.'

'Was he?'

'Sure how would I know? Most people say not, a harmless lad that was courting his girl on the bridge, without minding anyone.'

'Then why did they attack him?'

'Why do you think? You know bloody well those boys don't need a reason for beating up one of our sort.'

'Maybe he had papers on him, or an explosive. After all, there's been a lot of trouble lately.'

In the preceding months, the IRA campaign against the North had been revived. It was the same sad old story, barracks, customs huts blown up, and police patrols ambushed. Several men had been killed on both sides, and the police force had been augmented, even in relatively quiet areas like Moorhill, which though predominantly Catholic, was too far from the border for a raiding party to risk. A hut at the end of the town had gone on fire one night, but it turned out to be some children playing a prank.

'Damn the explosive he had with him, except,' his father smiled thinly, 'you count the girl. But those bloody B-Specials are so anxious to prove their importance, strutting around the town with their wee guns. Besides, they're shitting their britches with fear and mad to get their own back.'

'I see.' Peter forbore from pointing out that some of these motives were mutually exclusive, recognising his father's mood only too well. He poured a last cup of tea.

'Well, what are you going to do about it?' said his father fiercely.

'What do you mean, what am I going to do?'

'You were talking last night about Englishmen and freedom. Well there's an example of your English freedom, and a fine sight it is. What are you going to do about it?'

'What do you want me to do? Look for a gun?' he said sardonically.

'You could do worse. But your sort would faint at the sight of one.'

Peter flared. 'Would we, indeed? Well, maybe we've seen too many, handled by the wrong people.'

'What the hell are you going to fight them with, then?' his father snorted. 'A pen-nib? A typewriter? A fat lot of use that would be against a Sten-gun.'

'It might be of more use than you think. Moral protest is always best, as Gandhi showed. But they did not teach you that in Ballykinlar internment camp.'

'Moral protest, me granny. How are you going to bring moral protest to bear on bucks like that? Force only recognises greater force.'

Peter Douglas rose and, placing his back against the rail of the stove, looked down at his father. The dark-blue pouches under his eyes, gorged with blood, the right arm raised as though to thump the table in affirmation: he could have been cast in bronze as The Patriot. His own limp ease, the horn-rimmed glasses, the scarf tucked in nearly at the throat of his sports-shirt, the pointed black Italian shoes — everything represented a reaction against this old fire-eater who had dominated his childhood like a thundercloud. But now he felt no fear of him, only a calm certainty of his own position.

'You know well, Father, in your heart of hearts, that violence is the wrong way. Now you ask me what I can do. Well, in this specific case, I can do more than you or a whole regiment of the IRA. I can write an article in *The Tocsin* which will expose the whole thing. Good, decent — yes, English — people will read it and be ashamed of what is being done in their name. Questions will be asked, maybe in Parliament, if not this time, then the next. And gradually, if they are shown the enormity of what they are doing, the ruling classes of Ulster will come to their senses. One cannot hope to survive in the twentieth century on the strength of a few outdated shibboleths: prejudice always breeds violence.'

His father was silent, whether impressed or not, Peter could not say. Then, rising to clear away the breakfast things, he said:

'You'll do that then. You'll write the article.'

'I will.'

His father smiled, cunningly. 'Well, at least I got you to do something. You haven't completely lost your Ulster spirit yet.'

Peter's first task was to collect the information. He began to move around the town, listening to conversations in shop and pub. At first he drew a blank; seeing him enter with his pale look, his city air, the men at the bar went silent or whispered among themselves. When they had established his identity ('O you're James Douglas's boy,' a double recognition of family and religion flooding across the face) they spoke again, angrily.

'Oh, the black boys gave him a good going over, like,' said one man with a knowing wink and nod. 'You don't get off lightly when you're in their hands.'

'Is he badly hurt?' asked Peter.

'Now I couldn't tell you that exactly, but the doctor was with him this morning. They say he has a broken arm, anyway.'

'I heerd he had two broken ribs and stetches in his head forby.'

'Oh, they gave him the stick all right.'

'You'll get no fair deal from the likes of them.'

'They're black as can be.'

But when Peter asked what was going to be done by way of protest, they looked at him bleakly, shaking their heads.

'Sure you know it's no bloody use,' said one, hopelessly.

'You'd be a marked man from that day out,' said another.

'Sure you know the black boys have it all sewn up,' said a third, joining the litany of defeat.

Their passivity only heightened Peter's resolution, the only thing troubling him being the lack of specific detail. Very few people seemed even to know the boy who lived far out, in the Black Mountain district. And those who did did not always approve of him; they said he was very 'close' and used to hang around the juke-box in Higgins' Café. Yet they were all agreed on the wanton brutality of the beating, though the majority confessed to having been too far away to see much.

The source for the earlier part of the story was the girl, but she had run away when the struggle started and her father had forbidden her to leave the house. Since the man whom Peter had seen rebuking the police was the schoolmaster, he would not be home until evening and the nearest to an eye-witness he could find was the owner of the Dew Drop Inn. He and his wife slept in a room overlooking the street, exactly where the worst of the struggle had taken part. Yes they had struck him a lot, he told Peter, but he had heard one of them say: 'To be sure and hit him round the body, it leaves less mark.'

'There should be a boycott against them bucks,' concluded the publican, grimly.

In The Mountain Rest, however, Peter found the town clerk calmly drinking a large whiskey. Tall, with a drooping sandy moustache, he had served in an artillery regiment during the Normandy campaign and the boyish vigour with which he propounded atheism in a community highly given to religious hypocrisy had always amused Peter. The clerk thought that what had happened the previous night was a storm in a tea-cup. The boy had been looking for trouble and the only mistake was that the police had not acted promptly enough. 'The only thing to do with a gulderer like that is to hit him on the head with a mallet: that puts a stop to the squealing!'

No one spoke. Gulping down his lager, Peter left: it was time to start his article.

It is depressing to encounter violence again, its familiar pattern of fear and impotence. The first time I met it was in New York: a huddle of boys under a street lamp and then the single figure staggering backwards, hands to his side, while the others fled. My first impulse was to help but a firm hand held me back. By the time the ambulance arrived, the boy was dead.

That is the classic scene of urban violence; the spectator is absolved in the sheer remoteness of the action. It is not quite so scenic when it happens among people one knows. Recently I returned to the small town in the North of Ireland . . .

Well, it was a beginning at least; a little academic in its irony, and the 'philosophical' lead-in would probably have to be scrapped; but still, a beginning. It would improve when he got down to the actual incident: should he begin with a description of the town to give the background, or should he just plunge in? And there would have to be interviews with the police especially — not used to being taken up, they would probably condemn themselves out of their own mouths.

As Peter hesitated, he heard someone enter the bedroom where he was sitting, his portable propped on a suitcase in front of him. It was his mother; she had a brightly fringed shawl around her shoulders and she was carrying a hotwater bottle. This she inserted into the bed, with great ostentation.

'I thought I'd put it in early this evening, and have the bed warm for you. It was pretty sharp last night.'

Peter waited impatiently for her to leave, but as she delayed, rearranging the sheet several times, it became obvious that the hot-water bottle was only an excuse.

'I see you're writing,' she said at last.

'Yes.'

'Is it about last night?'

'More or less.'

'I suppose it was him put you up to it.' She always referred to his father in this semi-abstract way, as if he were not so much her husband as someone who had been wished on her years ago, a regrettable but unchanging feature of the household.

'More or less. But I would probably have done it myself in any case.'

'Do you think it's a sensible thing to do?'

'How do you mean, sensible? One can't let things like that pass without protest.

She looked at him in silence for a few moments and then, placing her hands on her hips, said: 'You're much better out of it. You'll only make trouble for all of us.'

'That's not what Father thinks.'

'I don't care what he thinks. I've lived with that man, God knows, for over thirty years and I still don't understand him. I think he never grew up.' She offered the last sentence with a grimace of half amused resignation.

'But I agree with him in this case.'

'Oh, it's easy for you. You don't live here all year round. That thing you're writing will create bad blood. I've seen too much fighting between neighbours in this town already.'

'But, Mother, you used to be a great rebel!' His father had often told, with great amusement, how she had been arrested for singing 'The Soldiers Song' on the beach at Warrenpoint; she had picked off the policeman's hat with her parasol and thrown it into the bathing pool. This incident was known in the family as Susie's fight for Irish Freedom.

'I've seen too much of it,' she said, flatly. 'My brothers fought for Irish Independence and where did it get them?

They're both in Australia now, couldn't get jobs in their own country. Look at you: when you want a job you have to go to England.'

'But I'm only writing an article, Mother, not taking up a gun.'

'It's all the same tune. Sour grapes and bad blood. It's me and him will have to live here if that thing appears, not you. Come down to your tea and leave that contraption alone.' She gestured towards the typewriter as if it were accursed.

Peter rose reluctantly. Despite her frail body, her china-pale complexion, her great doll's eyes, she had the will of a dragon. During the next few days, mysterious references to this article would crop up again and again in her conversation, references designed to make his father and himself feel uneasy, like guilty schoolboys.

'But surely you don't approve of what they did?' he said.

'Approve of them, of course I don't. They're a bad lot.' Muttering she disappeared into the kitchen, to reappear with an egg-whisk and a bowl of eggs. 'But we have to live with them,' she announced, driving the egg-whisk into the eggs like an electric drill. 'Why else did God put them there?'

IV

One must distinguish between the Royal Ulster Constabulary and the familiar English 'bobby'. The Ulster police are the only ordinary police, in these islands, to carry revolvers; during times of Emergency, they are armed with Sten-guns. Add to that 12,000 B-Specials and you have all the elements of a police state — not in Spain or South Africa, but in the British Isles. Such measures are not, as is argued, preventive, but the symptoms of political disease.

Police! Peter Douglas never knew a moment when he had not feared and detested them. It was partly his father's example: walking with him through the town, as a child, or on the way out to the chapel, he would feel him stiffen when a black uniform came in sight. If a constable, new to the place, dared salute him, he would gaze through him with a contemptuous eye. It was also the uniform; the stifling black of the heavy serge, the great belt, above all the dark bulk of the holster riding the hip: the archetypal insignia of brutality and repression. There was one, in particular, who was known as 'the storm-trooper': a massive ex-commando, he strode around the town with a black police dog, padding at his heels. He had long left the district, but for Peter Douglas, he had become the symbol of all the bitterness of his native province, patrolling for ever the lanes of Ulster, as dark and predatory as the beast at his side.

And then there were the Special police, young locals, issued with rifles and Sten-guns, and handsomely paid for night duty. The first time Peter had seen them he was about ten years old, cycling home one warm summer evening from his uncle's house in Altamuskin. There were about thirty, drilling before a tin-roofed Orange Lodge. Although he knew most of them, local Protestants whom he had met in shop or street, or in whose farmhouses he had been, they ignored him, gazing bleakly forward. Three nights later, they had stopped him and his father at a street corner, and, pretending not to recognise them, held them up for nearly half an hour.

Darkly unjust these memories might be, Peter Douglas reflected as he walked down the street, but the events of the previous night seemed to bear them out. From Higgin's Café came a gush of light and music, the harsh sound of a pop-record. Under the circle of a street light stood the diminutive figure of Joe Doom, the village idiot, eating from one of his tin cans. A group of children surrounded him, but they shrank back into the dark as Peter passed.

Outside the barracks itself, on a hillock at the end of the town, there appeared to be an unusual amount of activity. There was a Land-Rover, containing several police, drawn up in front, together with a long black car the wireless antennae and the dark glittering body of which unmistakably proclaimed a squad car. The barracks was a large building, painted in panels of white outlined with black; without the blue police sign over the door, it might have been a doctor's or a company director's house in some comfortable English suburb. But, surrounded on every side by great rolls of barbed wire and with a sandbag blockhouse, from the slit of which protruded a machine-gun, it looked like a fortress, the headquarters of the Gauleiter in an occupied town. As he came up the path, he saw a flash of movement in the blockhouse; he was being kept under cover.

'Is the Sergeant in?' Peter asked. And then, irritably: 'For God's sake, put that thing down. I live up the street.'

'What do ye want with him?' A young constable emerged, the Sten-gun dangling on his arm, insubstantial in its menace as a Meccano toy.

'I'd like to interview him. I'm a journalist and I work for a paper in England. I'd like to discuss the incident last night with him.'

'You're a journalist,' said the constable, with an intonation of flat incredulity. 'In England?'

'Yes, and I'd like to see the Sergeant, please.'

There was a moment's silence, while the policeman looked at him, his eyes pale blue and vacant in a dead-white face, emphasised by the black peak of the cap. Then he turned and motioned Peter to follow him into the dayroom.

There were five men in the room, two local policemen whom he vaguely recognised, two rather sulky-looking

B-Specials and a fifth, who, by his bearing, tailored uniform with Sam Browne belt and polished leggings, seemed to be a superior officer. They looked surprised to see Peter.

'There's a man here, Sergeant,' said the Constable, addressing one of the local policemen, 'says he's a journalist. He works for some paper, in England.'

The Sergeant came forward, slowly. 'You're Mr Douglas's son, aren't you?' he asked, with a mixture of civility and doubt.

'Yes, Sergeant, I am. I work for a paper in England and I'm home on a short holiday. I'd like to get a few facts from you about the incident last night.'

'Last night?' The Sergeant looked in half desperation towards the well dressed officer.

'Which paper do you work for?' said the latter in a crisp voice. As he spoke, he came forward to face Peter as if by his presence hoping to subdue the intruder. It was the unmistakable voice of authority, British and chilling, as level in tone as a BBC announcer's.

Peter explained, politely.

'Yes, I see,' said the officer, noncommittally. 'I think I know the paper.' Then, to the Sergeant: 'Don't you think we should bring Mr Douglas into another room, Knowles?'

As Peter followed Sergeant Knowles into a large room at the back of the barracks, a thought struck him.

'That's the County Inspector, isn't it?'

'It is indeed,' said the Sergeant. He looked as if he wanted to say more but thought better of it, poking the fire for an instant in an aimless way, before leaving the room. So that was it: they were definitely troubled about the incident last night and the County Inspector had come down in person to investigate. He was on the right track after all.

The Chief Inspector entered the room briskly a few moments later. Planting himself luxuriously in front of the fire, he

turned to Peter with a bright energetic smile. Thin hair
brushed back above his ears, a long oval face with neatly divided moustache, lean-bridged nose and almost slanted eyes,
he was decidedly handsome, a man born and used to command.

'Well, now, Mr Douglas, it's not often we get one of you
chaps knocking around this part of the country. Sorry I can't
offer you a drink, but I doubt if the facilities of the barracks
are supposed to rise to that.' He laughed briefly. 'You're a
local man, I take it.'

'Yes,' said Peter. The bright offensiveness of the man's
tone angered, but also cowed him, so that, almost against his
will, he found himself volunteering further information. 'But I
went to school in Laganbridge.'

'Oh,' said the Inspector with interest, sensing common
ground. 'Went to school there myself. The Kings, I suppose.'

'No,' said Peter shortly. Then — incredulity merging into
satisfaction at the unexpected trap into which the Inspector
had fallen, deceived by the British sound of Douglas and the
fact that *The Tocsin* was a London paper — he added, 'St
Kieran's.'

It was like confessing, Peter thought with a smile, to an un-
reconstructed Southerner that though one looked quite normal,
one really was a Negro. The Kings was one of the most famous Protestant schools in the North of Ireland, a Georgian
nursery for cricketers, colonial administrators, gaitered bishops and even (as though to demonstrate its all round ability) a
distinguished literary critic. On the hill opposite, sheltering
under the great bulk of the post-Emancipation cathedral, was
the diocesan seminary of St Kieran's where the sons of strong
Catholic farmers, publicans and merchants studied, mainly for
the priesthood.

'Oh.' The Chief Inspector paused. Then, with a gallant return to self-possession: 'Used to know your Bishop a bit. Nice old chap. Don't fancy his taste in sherry much, though.'

'His sherry?' echoed Peter in amazement.

'Myas.' The way he pronounced it, with a prefatory hum and a hissing follow through, it could have been anything from 'my ears' to 'my arse'. 'Gets his shipped direct from Spain; our boys see it through the Customs for him. Bit dry. Prefer Bristol Cream myself.'

If such a man thought about Nationalists at all, it was probably as some obscure form of trouble-making minority; he did not mind contact with them providing it took place on the highest level, a Maharajah or a bishop, or some complaisant highly placed native official. And why should he change? Convinced of his tolerance, assured of his position within the framework of Queen and Country, he would probably end his days in honourable retirement with a minor decoration in the Honours List.

'I never met the Bishop,' Peter said curtly.

He might have saved his breath, the irony of his remark falling like a paper dart from that unruffled brow. The Inspector had already moved on.

'Well,' he said, 'about that little matter you mentioned. Don't think there's much in it for a fellow like you. Pretty small beer after all. Some young thug cheeked our boys and they took him in for a few hours to cool off. Released him in the morning. Routine affair.'

'After beating him up on the way,' Peter said stubbornly.

'Oh, I wouldn't say that,' said the Inspector, judiciously. 'He did resist arrest after all, so they had to help him along a bit. May have got a few scratches, but that would be the height of it.'

'Enough to put him in a hospital bed.'

'Oh, you heard that, did you?' the Inspector said with interest. 'Well, well, it's wonderful how rumours get round, though I'm afraid you won't find much substance in that one. Chap kept complaining so we called the doctor. He couldn't find much wrong with him but just to be on the safe side he sent him down to the County for an X-ray. Released in a few hours, right as rain. Mother came to bring him home'

'So you mean it was all nothing?' asked Peter, incredulously.

'Pretty well.'

'But the noise woke up the whole town.'

The Inspector laughed dryly. 'Yes, that was rather a nuisance. Chap was a bit of an exhibitionist. Roared like a bull, boys said, every time they laid a finger on him. Pretty cute trick when you come to think of it.'

'Trick?' Peter stared at the bland face opposite him. But he found neither deception nor doubt in the Inspector's level gaze.

'Yes, a trick. Can't be up to some of these fellows. Bit of a Teddy boy by all accounts, likes to show he's not afraid of the police. But I think he realises he went a bit too far last night, made a fool of himself.' The Inspector rubbed his hands together in a gesture of satisfied dismissal. 'Well, there you are, there's the whole little story. Sorry I can't provide something more juicy for you. I know what you Johnnies like. Perhaps next time.'

Stunned, Peter followed him along the corridor and out through the door. He was half-way up Main Street before he realised that the IRA had not even been mentioned.

'So that's what he said to you,' said the schoolmaster admiringly. Peter had called on him on his way home and they had crossed the street to the nearest pub, the Dew Drop Inn.

'Yes. I'm afraid I was so taken aback I couldn't think of anything to say. I mean, it all sounded so plausible; maybe the man was telling the truth.'

'Still, that doesn't explain why he called upon me.'

'Oh, did he, indeed?' breathed Peter.

'Yes, when I drove in from school, there was His Nibs waiting in the parlour. Said he often heard my brother who works in the County Health Office speak of me and thought he should drop by. Then, cool as you please, mentioned the business last night and said I would be glad to hear it had all been a misunderstanding. They had given the boy a good talking to and sent him home. There was no further reason for me to be troubled *in any way*. Special Constable Robson was sorry for what he had said to me, but it was all in the heat of the moment and meant nothing.'

'So they *were* troubled. . . . And what did you say?'

'What could I say? I just smiled back and said I accepted Robson's apologies and was glad to hear the boy was all right. I work here you know and so — as he delicately pointed out — does my brother. Besides' — he blinked nervously and hunched his narrow raincoated shoulders forward — 'I've been thinking the matter over and it seems to me we're not on very safe ground.'

'What do you mean? Surely a civilised man cannot let someone be beaten up under his eyes without protesting.'

'In an ordinary case, no. But the boy doesn't seem to have been badly hurt and we wouldn't be able to prove anything definite. We'd only be playing into their hands by showing ourselves as trouble makers.'

Peter was silent for a moment, sipping his lager. 'That's more or less what my mother says,' he said eventually, 'but not my father.'

'Your father, if you don't mind me saying so, is nearly as thick as an Orangeman in his own way. His kind of talk may be fair enough in Dáil Éireann, but as you know yourself, it cuts very little ice here. After all, even if we did get a United Ireland we would still have to live with them so we'd better start now. And you must admit the police in the North have had a pretty rough time lately. If this was the 'twenties, there'd be a lot of dead Tagues around.'

'So you think I should drop the article I'm doing?'

'Oh, I don't know, that depends. Why don't you go and see the boy before deciding? After all, he was the one who was beaten up.'

The owner of the Dew Drop Inn peered hurriedly round the door. 'Come on, gentlemen, please,' he said. 'It's half an hour after the time already.' As they passed through the kitchen on their way out, a group of men were on their way in. They were the B-Specials Peter had seen at the barracks. 'Good night now, Mr Concannon, good night, Mr Douglas,' the owner said as he shepherded them through the door. Then he turned to greet his new customers.

V

'That must be it,' said James Douglas, craning across the shoulder of the hackney cab driver. For ten minutes or so, ever since they had left the main road, they had been bumping along a narrow country lane. At first there were signs of habitation, but as they wound their way up the mountainside, first the houses and then the trees began to fall away, long stretches of melancholy bog opening up on either side. At last, just as the gravel surface of the lane began to merge into the muddy ruts of a cart track, they caught sight of a small cottage. Whitewashed, with a greening thatched roof, it stood on a mound, without any shelter or protection from the wind except a rough fence, hammered out of old tar-barrels. Against the wall, its front wheel almost blocking the half-door, was a battered racing bicycle, painted a bright red.

'That's it, right enough,' said the driver. 'Any bids?'

'It looks bleak all right,' said Peter.

'Hungry's the word,' said the driver cheerfully, as he applied the hand brake.

'Do you want me to come with you?' his father asked, looking at Peter doubtfully. All the way to Black Mountain he had been humming to himself, in evident satisfaction, but the sight of the cottage seemed to have unnerved him.

'No,' said Peter shortly. 'I'll go myself.'

The swaying progress of the car up the lane had already attracted attention: a brown and white mongrel dog came racing down to greet it, and the startled face of a woman flashed briefly at one of the two small windows. As Peter descended from the car, his thin shoes sinking in the mud of the yard, the dog plunged towards him.

'Down, Flo, down.' A woman of about fifty, wearing a shapeless red jumper and a pair of thongless man's boots, appeared in the doorway. She stood, drying her hands in the corner of her discoloured apron, and waiting for Peter to speak.

'Does Michael Ferguson live here?'

A look of dismay, animal, uncomprehending, passed over her face. 'God protect us,' she muttered, 'more trouble.' Then, turning towards the door: 'He's in there, if you want him.'

After the light of the mountainside, the interior of the cottage seemed dim as a cave. A crumbling turf-fire threw a fitful smoky light over the hunched up figure of an old man who looked up as the intruder entered and then, with a noisy scraping of his stool, turned away. Beside the kettle in the ashes lay a sick chicken, its scrawny red head projecting from a cocoon of flannel. The other side of the room was taken by a cupboard and a bed upon which a young man was lying. There was a bandage round his forehead.

'Can't you rise, at laste, when someone comes to see you?' said the woman, gruffly.

The young man raised himself stiffly from the bed. He was about twenty, tall and rather well-built with broad shoulders. He wore an imitation leather jacket, heavy with metal buckles and clasps. It rode high above his waist, exposing a torn khaki shirt. This was stuffed loosely into a pair of threadbare jeans, supported by a studded leather belt with a horseshoe buckle. The outfit was completed by bright blue- and red-ribbed socks above the black heaviness of farm boots.

'Are you police?' His eyes, close-set in a face heavily blotched with acne, avoided Peter's; he could have been speaking to the dog which by now whined and twined around his legs.

Peter explained as best he could. In his nervousness, he found himself using words that, by the puzzled expression in their faces, he knew they could not understand, so he repeated his story several times. 'I want to help, you see,' he ended.

'I don't think I can do much for you, mister,' the boy said, at last.

'What do you mean, you can't do much for me? That's not the point at all. I want to do something for you. I want to write an article that will expose the way you have been treated by the police. You don't mean to say you haven't been beaten up?'

From the hearth behind came an unexpected sound as the old man swivelled on his stool. His eyes, small and red-rimmed as a turkey cock's, were bright with venom, and as he spoke a streak of spittle ran down the front of his collarless shirt.

'If he'd stayed home with his mother the way a dacent-rared boy should, not a hate would have happened him. But nothing for it nowadays but running off to the pictures and the music boxes. He deserved all he got, and not half good enough for him, hell slap it up him!'

The boy's face flushed, but he remained silent. Instead, his mother spoke for him.

'To tell the truth, sir, we'd as lief the matter was forgotten. It would be better for all of us, like.'

'That's right, sir. The way it is, I wouldn't make too much of it, sir.'

So there it was, plain as a pikestaff. The police had spoken not merely to the boy, but also to the mother. They were quite prepared for the boy's sake and the sake of his parents that the matter should be overlooked; in their magnanimity, they had probably provided transport, an impossible expense, otherwise, for people in their position. Whatever redress Peter could offer, whatever hope or help would mean nothing compared to their unspecified but real threats. He would never know the truth of the incident now: whether the boy had connections with the IRA, whether he had provoked the police; whether even, his — Peter's — interpretation of their silence was correct. Between their helplessness and his freedom lay an unbridgeable gulf and, with a despairing gesture, he turned to leave. The boy and his mother accompanied him; the former, despite half-hearted attempts to conceal it, had a distinct limp.

'I'm sorry I can't help you now, sir,' he said. His voice, though flat in tone, sounded almost kindly. As he bent his head under the door, Peter noticed that, above the bandage, his hair was plastered back in two oily swathes, like the wings of a duck.

As the Austin 10 lurched down the mountainside, Peter and his father were both silent. A storm cloud was gathering over the valley, dark as a shawl. Only the driver seemed in a jaunty mood, as he expanded on the history of the Fergusons for their benefit.

'He's not a bad lad that, you know,' he said reflectively, 'rough and all as he is. The two other boys, cute enough, sloped off to England. He was in Barnsley too, but he came back when the old man had the operation. There's many wouldn't do it.'

It was only when they had reached home that James Douglas spoke, climbing laboriously through the door his son was holding for him, onto the kerb.

'Are you still going to write that article?' he asked apprehensively, peering into Peter's face.

Peter looked at him for a moment, as though in calculation.

'I don't really know,' he said.

. . . There is a way of dealing with such incidents of course, familiar to every colonial officer from Ulster to Rhodesia. The charge is dropped or minimised, the too zealous police or soldiers reprimanded, any public fuss avoided. Perhaps as the authorities claim, it is the best way in the end. But one is left wondering in how many small Ulster towns such things are happening, at this moment, in your name!

After his return, Peter had gone straight to his bedroom to continue the article, with little success. He could not even decide, staring blankly at the paragraph he had just written, whether to give it up or not: he could get a beginning and an end, but the whole thing did not cohere into the cry, logical but passionate, for which he had been hoping. He rose to pace the room; finally, he found himself at the window, vacantly looking out down Main Street, as he had done on that first night.

It had been raining heavily for an hour or so, but now it was clearing. On the rim of the sky, just to the west of the town, a watery sun was breaking through grey clouds. Soft, almost a dawn light, it shone on the town, making the long line of the main Street, from the Old Tower to the War Memorial and beyond to the railway station, seem washed and clear.

There it was, his home town, laid out before him, bright in every detail. He knew every corner of it, had gone to school in that low concrete building, run his sleigh down that hill, had even, later, brought his first girl down the darkness of that entry. He knew every house and nearly everybody in them. One did not like or dislike this place: such emotions were irrelevant, it was part of one's life, and therefore inescapable. Yet all through his final year at school his only thought had been to escape; the narrowness of the life, the hidden bitterness of political feeling had suddenly seemed like the régime of a prison. The Irish were supposed to be a merry race, but there was something in Ulster people, a harsh urge to reduce the human situation to its barest essentials, which frightened him. It was years before he had felt able to come back, sufficiently secure in his own beliefs to be able to survive the hostility their ways seemed to radiate.

But did that strength now give him the right to sit in judgement, particularly where an incident like this was concerned? Already, only two days afterwards, indignation had died down in the town. Was it fear or an effort to foster that good will which people like his mother thought was the only solution? Or mere passivity, the product of a commercial spirit which saw everyone as a potential customer? Whatever destiny lay in these grey walls, they might surely be left to work out on their own, two peoples linked and locked for eternity.

As he looked over the town, sober with self-judgement, suddenly from out of a lane-way, as though propelled, shot a dwarf-like figure. His clothes were of various colours, and he wore a tattered cap pulled squarely over his ears. One foot was bare, the other encased in an elderly boot. Around his waist hung a bandolier of tin-cans. Peter recognised him almost at once: it was Joe Doom, the village idiot. He lived in a tiny house on his own, at the end of the town, begging pennies from passers-by, stewing scraps in his tin cans. The people teased him, fed him, tolerated him, with a charity older than state institutions, and in return, his antics, the gargles and lapses of logic which were his sole method of speech, amused them. Now he looked wildly around, at the sky, at the watery sun, at the light shining on the fronts of the houses. Then, as though focusing, he saw Peter at the window above him. Their eyes met for a moment and something like triumph entered Joe Doom's. He fumbled frantically behind his back, the line of cans shaking, and produced a piece of white cardboard. With a quick glance behind him towards the entry, as though for confirmation, he held it high above his head, so that Peter — and anyone else in the street who was watching — could read. In large crude letters, like slashes of charcoal, it spelt

Nosy Parker
Go home

1963

The Road Ahead

WE MET half-way down where the steep hill used to be. He was on his way up, pushing a bicycle, I was walking down. The traffic had been so heavy that I had taken the mountain lane (the old grass-grown detour farmers used when driving their cattle to the fair) and was only now re-emerging onto the bright macadam. The new road was lined, for the sake of visibility, with a white stone border, and it was just inside that he was walking, with the bicycle wheels over the edge.

We saw each other at a distance, and had time to prepare our responses, though now and again cars came whipping past to obscure the view. I had not expected him to recognise me, but he did, stopping when we came abreast, at different sides of the road.

'Hallo, there,' he called expectantly.

There was no point in trying to talk so far apart so I waited for a moment until the traffic eased, and then sprinted across.

'Hallo, yourself,' I said.

He stood looking at me, with his elbow propped on the worn heart shape of the bicycle saddle. The left eye was as bad as ever, watery and unfocused, with (if you could look closely without flinching) the eyeball lying in its cradle of pink blood. He had got it working with barbed wire, and it had never been looked after. It gave him a baleful look which he was not above exploiting; like the cripple who offers his maimed right hand only to friends, he would watch steadily, daring you to drop your gaze.

'There's a queer change,' he said, indicating the road.

Just then a Ford and Vauxhall came around the corner, locked in speed. We watched them meet the slight incline of the hill, without checking, and then zoom past. The Ford, which was on the inside, was so close to the shoulder of the road that it sent up a shower of pebbles that rang on the bicycle frame. But it did not yield, and we watched them disappear into the distance, like two runners between the narrowing white tapes of the stone border.

'Aye, there's a change,' I said.

We remained in restful silence, looking at each other (with the half-smile of people exchanging friendly, but unstated memories) for a minute or two. Then he shifted and I saw it was time to speak again.

'Still you take the bicycle,' I ventured.

'It's better than nothing for them that's poor.' Then he grinned. 'But they got me in the end.'

'How so?'

'I was coming by MacCrystals, pushing hard to get a bit of a run up the hill. Not that there's much of a slope now, but if you have the habit ...' He paused.

'Well?'

'There was a bus behind me, one of those big city double-deckers they use now to bring the schoolchildren home. That was bad enough but then (you can see nearly half a mile now, you know) a big brute of a CALCO oil-tanker came sailing over the crest. The bus nearly had me in the ditch as it was, but when I saw the other buck, I said to myself, John Mooney, you should know when you're beat. I declare to God a midge couldna passed between them.'

Though he made light of it, I saw that the incident had depressed him, and hastened to add an interested comment.

'It reminds me of the war.'

'How, like?'

'You remember when the American troops were training here, and used to stage manoeuvres? I came out of school one day, and found a whole armoured column on the road: one of the Shermans went over the ditch around here. We had to go home round the lane, just as I did today. I suppose you might say that the war never ended here!'

But he was in no mood for my pompous theories, and stood looking at the road.

'Do you know what it is,' he said suddenly. 'I'm often sorry I didn't go 'way, like yourself. As it is, I don't know sometimes whether I'm here, or someplace else. Only last night, when I was coming back from Donnelly's after a few drinks, I declare to my God, I got lost. . . .' There was such a depth of terror in the one good eye that all I could do was change the subject.

'Is that MacCrystals you mentioned the people who have the shop?' Not that I didn't remember it well; it was half-way on my three-mile walk from school, and we would stop to buy lollipops. Or drink from the clear spring that ran under the elm tree at the other side of the road.

'They sell the odd sweetie,' he said indifferently.

We stood side by side, looking at the landscape. Something curious about the quality of the silence struck me: I could not hear a single bird. There were no hedgerows any more, they had been bulldozed to level the ditch on either side, and lengthen the view. So there was nothing between us and the small, damp fields but the metal fence, supported every now and then by concrete posts, inset with cat's-eye reflectors.

'Did you have a drink at the spring?' I tried again.

'Spring!' he said incredulously. 'God look to your wit; sure they scared the water back into the ground again!'

The phrase seemed to please him, for he laughed shortly and changed the subject.

'Do you know MacNeils?' he demanded, naming another shop about three miles down the road.

'Why?'

'It's up for auction.'

I waited, to see his face turn directly towards me again. I had never noticed before the contrast between the bad eye, and the hesitant, almost tremulous mouth below, like a mournful horse.

'Do you know why that house fell?'

'Why?'

'There was a beggar woman by the name of Meanens lived in a wee hut on that land; she had a coupla weans and some say old MacNeil himself fathered the last. But there was one winter so hard that even the river froze; she came down to the shop every day, looking for scraps, until they had to drive her away. And when they refused her, she stood on the hill, with her children around her, and took the rosary beads from her pocket ...'

It is Christmas. On a white hill, a ragged Snow Queen stands, a child at her breast, a dog at her heels. Below lie the few houses of the village, mysterious as a crystal ball, under the drifting snow. She takes from her apron a bag of Fox's Glacier Mints, and a pair of horn rosary beads to which a sweet paper clings. She begins to intone.

Down in the village shop, the light of the Calor gas lamp shines on ruddy flitches of bacon, crusty soda farls, and Tate and Lyles fine powdered sugar. As the grocer fills brown paper bags, he talks to his customers, and laughs the laugh of the well-fed. He is a small man, clad in a brown dustcoat: there is a white pollen of flour on his eyelashes. Little busy bee, he seems oblivious of his danger: only the collie dog lying with crossed paws at the door scents something, and rises, hackles bristling before the supernatural.

'And from that day to this there has been a curse on that place.'

Giddy with nausea, I wrench myself back to consciousness; whom have I been talking to, and where? Luckily, a rattling lorry is drawing up: I recognise the contractor who lives across from us. That house also had a bad name, a tubercular family having wasted in it. For years it stood deserted, except for the cattle that sheltered in the kitchen or the bats that looped through the empty windows. Now he had rebuilt the grey walls, and is flattening the field before the house to make an avenue. He is offering us both a lift; I help my companion to put his bicycle in the back, where it rests with the front wheel lightly spinning.

'You're not coming,' he says, with one foot on the running board.

'I'll go on ahead yet.'

'Take care of yourself,' the one good eye winks ferociously through the rectangle of the window.

One hundred yards further down the hill, I reach the spring. It is true that they have done something to it: the tree is gone, and a white concrete wall has been constructed, to support the empty space of the ditch. But there is a kind of porthole, through which a trickle is coming. I kneel down, on one knee, to put my hands under it. How strange that a spring should flow opposite a house called MacCrystals, a sign of that magic congruence that rules so many aspects of life. . . .

It took nearly five minutes for the cup of my palms to fill. Then I bent my head, and took an expectant gulp. It tasted sour, brackish, as though strained through metal. Turning my hands over slowly, I let it drain to the ground.

A Change of Management

9.50 a.m.
JOHN O'SHEA groaned as he lifted the morning paper from
the front of his desk, where his secretary, Nan Connor, had left
it. He was already in a bad temper (for the second time that
week he had got snarled in a traffic jam on his way in from
Clontarf) but what he saw on the front page did not help. That
bastard Clohessy was in the news again; chubby and smiling,
an assuring blend of episcopal dignity and *bon viveur's*
charm, his face seemed to start out from the lead photograph
with the immediacy of a film star's. Among the dignitaries at
the blessing of the dried-vegetable factory were the Most Rev.
Dr Martin, Bishop of Avoca, the Most Rev. Dr Nkomo, Vicar
Apostolic of Katanga (a fine tall African, nurtured by Irish
nuns) and Dr William Pearse Clohessy. At a dinner in the
Leinster Hotel afterwards, Dr Clohessy, Chairman of *Bord na
h-Ath Breithe*, The National Renaissance Board, said that this
new factory, for which they had all worked so hard, represented another beam in the scaffolding of Ireland's future.

Another nail in its coffin, more likely, thought O'Shea,
nearly disintegrating with rage as he gazed at the picture of
the new factory which headed the Advertising Supplement. A
long low building, it seemed to consist mainly of glass, acres
of it, with intersecting ridges of concrete creating a pattern
grid. Surely normal people would not be expected to work in a
chilly barracks like that, which looked as if it were designed
for Martians. He looked to the side for space vehicles, but all
he could see was a car park, with the Tricolour flying, against
a background of mountains. We congratulate the architect,

said Dr Clohessy, on his revolutionary conception, which liberates the forces implicit in the building's environment, so that employees will have the sensation of working close to nature, without its disadvantages. The stark beauty of its outline challenges nature's ruggedness in the granite majesty of the Wicklow Mountains.

As O'Shea was dwelling with tortured relish on the idea of granite majesty, and wondering which of Clohessy's team of ghost-writers had dreamt it up, the door of his office opened and his secretary came in. 'Here are the letters, Mr O'Shea,' she said, placing a small pile of opened envelopes on the IN tray to the right of his desk. She stood back, smoothing her skirt with a broad hand, as he ruffled them. 'Will you be wanting me?' she asked, at last, with unconscious generosity, gazing over his head through the window.

'Is there anything urgent?'

'The Chairman wants to see you at eleven; his secretary rang to confirm the appointment. I believe the Efficiency Experts are due soon.'

'Anything else?'

She hesitated. 'Mr Cronin called.'

'What did he want?'

'He said you were to meet him for lunch in the Anchor.'

As always she delivered the message with a disapproving air, as if she felt that he should not be going to places like the Anchor, especially with people like Tadgh Cronin. Nan Connor was a decent, middle-class Dublin woman, and there were certain classes of behaviour which she could not admire. Once when she had tried to stall Cronin, saying that Mr O'Shea was engaged, he had broken into a torrent of bad language. 'Will you get that bastard for me, or I'll come and wrap your guts around a lamppost,' he finished. The girls at the switchboard had laughed, but she had not found it amusing; and she never would.

John O'Shea smiled affectionately after her, as her masculine shoulders disappeared through the door. Whoever had dreamt up 'granite majesty' should have known Nan Connor; there was something heart-warning about people who behaved according to form. He reached for the first file on his desk and began to turn its pages thoughtfully. It was ten-fifteen, and all across Claddagh House the typewriters took up their morning song.

MEMORANDUM: ON THE HISTORY OF CLADDAGH HOUSE

Claddagh House was a handsome building, of port-wine brick, standing on the South Side of Dublin, near the river Dodder. Formerly known as Kashmir House, it had been built by a retired Army Officer at the turn of the century. But the family had left after the Revolution, no longer finding life comfortable in Ireland, and the house had changed hands several times. After a period as divisional headquarters of the Boys Scouts (Dublin Brigade) it had caught the eye of a government minister, who was looking for somewhere to house an offshoot of his department. Since money was scarce, no effort was made to remodel it; the stuffed tiger heads of the original owner still lined the entrance hall, and in the Chairman's room hung two crossed assegais, with the head of an eland between them.

What pleased John O'Shea about Claddagh House was its Victorian spaciousness; it was unashamedly designed to be lived in. A militant laurel hedge protected it from the road, too high for the curious, but just enough for the occupants to command both directions. There were two pillared entrances, through which one could sweep, the car coming to a halt before the door with a satisfying spurt of gravel. A well tended lawn began at the side of the house, coming to a climax in the tree-shadowed expanse at the back.

The front was dominated by two enormous bay windows, a flight of steps between them mounting to the door, with its well Brassoed-knocker and official plaque. John O'Shea still remembered the first day he had penetrated the grave dignity of that façade. A junior civil servant, he had just been seconded to Claddagh House, and did not know what to expect. He stood at the empty reception desk in the hall, under the stuffed animals, with their bared teeth and eyeballs. The only sound in the building seemed to be coming from underneath the stairs.

When he opened the door and saw the crowd around a table he nearly backed out, thinking he had interrupted a conference. Then he recognised the object in the middle of the table: from a battered looking radio rose the florid accents of a racing commentator.

They're coming into the bend now, King's Pin in front, Whistling Nun second, Richards nursing Champagne Paddy on the rails. AND here we come into the straight. It's still King's Pin; but Whistling Nun is challenging. I say, this is something; King's Pin, Whistling Nun and Champagne Paddy neck and neck. TWO furlongs to go and King's Pin is falling back; it's between Whistling Nun and Champagne Paddy. ONE furlong and Richards' mount is beginning to flag; it's Whistling Nun all the way now — WHISTLING NUN BY A LENGTH!

11 a.m.

After ten years, John O'Shea still found that first view of Claddagh House prophetic. It was not that work did not get done, but that it took its own sweet pace, without the panic of a central department. Files accumulated and were dealt with as they simmered into urgency. Then they were tied in red folders and buried in cupboards as large as bank-vaults.

And there was always time for relaxation. Twice daily they assembled in the old kitchen under the stairs for tea. In the summer they could take their work out onto the lawn; O'Shea had been sitting under a lilac tree when a swallow dunged on a letter from the Department of Finance. Everyone contributed to the typists' Black Babies Fund; everyone went off sugar and milk during Lent; everyone joined in the Staff Dance and Annual Outing.

Which was why he found the timing of his appointment with the Chairman curious: if he was holding it during the tea-break, it was because he wanted no one to interrupt them. And that was unlike Jack Donovan, who gave the impression of conducting his business in public. His gregarious vagueness masked a veteran shrewdness; he might be late but he was rarely wrong in a decision. From ten-thirty when he rolled in to consult the rain gauge, until he left for his game of golf in the afternoon, he refused to be hustled by or for anything.

As John O'Shea opened the door (after a polite knock) he caught the sharp odour of the cigars Donovan favoured. On one of the eland's horns a hat was hanging: it gave the animal a querulous, lopside look. Donovan himself was at his desk, a plump tweed-suited man, who raised his head cordially to indicate a chair. Rejecting the open box of Will's cheroots which his Chairman pushed towards him, O'Shea settled himself expectantly.

'You wanted to see me, sir?'

As usual, Donovan took his time to answer, tidying the papers on his desk before leaning back, his fingers joined.

'Yes, indeed,' he said. 'I have a job for you. Rather, I have two jobs; or one job with two aspects.'

O'Shea waited politely for clarification.

'There's a dinner tonight in' — he pulled a piece of paper towards him — 'the Royal Hotel, Carricklone, which I am supposed to attend: they're launching a local development plan. But . . .'

'You would rather I did.' Which was it, this time, yachting or golf? Since it was mid-week, it was probably golf, as his favourite seaside course, near Bray.

Donovan smiled. 'That's right. But not for the reason you think, though I do have a previous engagement. In any case, even if I was free, I think you should go. You see, Clohessy will be there.'

John O'Shea started. 'That . . .' he began automatically.

'I'm not sure that I don't share your impatience with Mr — Dr! — Clohessy: he seems a rather pushy fellow,' said Donovan judiciously. 'But one mustn't reply on spot judgements; he has the reputation of being very capable. Which brings me to the second part . . .'

'I hope it has nothing to do with Clohessy,' O'Shea burst in.

'Well, as a matter of fact, in a sort of a roundabout way, it has. You know that the Minister feels that perhaps we should be reorganised. It's partly a political thing, of course — we were founded by the previous government — but they also feel that perhaps we are a little old-fashioned. You've heard the Efficiency Experts are coming in . . .'

'Miss Connor said they were due next week.'

'They're only a front, of course. I don't mean that they won't do their — whatever they do — conscientiously, but their report will give an official reason for pointing out something that we all know already: that this is not a very modern organisation, and that I'm not a very modern manager.

'I don't think that's so important, sir,' said O'Shea loyally.

Donovan wheeled his chair slightly, so that he was gazing through the window. On the green pelt of the lawn, a solitary blackbird was trying to extricate a worm; when it succeeded, it nearly fell backwards, the worm projecting like a typewriter ribbon from its beak.

'I'm a bumbler,' he said quietly, 'and the age of bumblers is past. But I was lucky; I managed to last until nearly retiring age. I'll be able to disappear without undue fuss.'

'Have you any idea of who might be replacing you?' asked O'Shea nervously.

It was a minute or two before Donovan answered. 'Yes,' he said heavily, 'I think I do. It's mainly guess-work on my part, coupled with one or two fairly obvious straws in the wind. But I think that not merely me, but also Claddagh House, are to be retired. There's going to be what the English papers call, I believe, a takeover bid.'

'By whom?'

'By Bord na h-Ath Breithe. They plan to pull down the house and set up a new joint building.'

'Under Clohessy?' breathed O'Shea.

'Under Clohessy.' Donovan swung the chair round so that he was facing O'Shea directly. 'That's why I want you to go to Carricklone. So that you can get a closer look at the man you may soon be working under.'

1 p.m.

Why did Tadgh Cronin always spend his lunch hour in the Anchor? As John O'Shea pushed open the heavy mahogany door, a hollow sound rose to greet him, like the sea booming in a cave. They were standing six deep at the bar, with waiters threading through the mass, carrying platters to the tables at the back. It was certainly not the food, because it was always cold, pallid thighs of chicken or rough cuts of ham and beef. It was certainly not the women because, although there were

several presentable girls present, they seemed to accept that
they were on sufferance and did their best to past muster as
men, sucking their pints slowly. A lecher would have had a
field-day, provided he remained sober enough to remember his
priorities.

No, the sole purpose of this draughty, uncomfortable high-
ceilinged place was drink. And with that O'Shea caught sight
of Tadgh Cronin, ensconced (his brooding posture demanded
the word) in a corner, under a vine-leaved mirror advertising
Guinness. His black steeple hat was on the chair beside him,
flanked by a crumpled *Irish Times*. As O'Shea sat down opposite, he saw that his face looked heavy and flushed, and that
the hand that reached out for the pint was shaking.

'Hard night?' he asked sympathetically.

Cronin turned an imploring eye towards heaven. 'Christ!'

Then, step by step, he began to piece together (as much for
his own sake as O'Shea's) the events of the previous night.
They had all been having a quiet jar in the Anchor when that
bastard Tomkins, the sculptor, barged in. A row had developed between him and Parsons, the stained-glass artist, and
they had all been thrown out. When they moved to some girl's
flat in Rathmines he, Cronin, had tried to make peace between
Tomkins and Parsons, with the result that they both turned on
him. A window had been broken, and when he got home at
four o'clock, he found he had been cheated by the taxi man.

O'Shea made another sympathetic noise; he had heard the
same story before but he had a connoisseur's taste for the
gruesome detail. How much had the fare been from Rathmines
to Ballsbridge?

'I got half a dollar back: that makes nearly a quid for two
miles. Over eight bob a fecking mile — you could fly
cheaper!'

Together, in gloomy silence, they surveyed the bar and its customers. A well-known actor was leaning at the counter, surrounded by a circle of admiring young men. When he saw Cronin, he bowed gracefully so that they could see the dark, corrugated lines of his wig. 'Did you make it to the office, at least?'

'I'm going in this afternoon. Old Brennan's beginning to get a big narky.'

Brennan was Cronin's immediate superior in the Department of Woods and Lakes. A harmless, long-suffering man, he not merely overlooked the fact that Cronin spent most of his time in the office studying form, or writing reviews for the daily papers, but even countenanced his long absences, periods when he disappeared underground, only to turn up looking as if he had been passed through a mangle. It was a combination of old-fashioned fidelity and the respect still paid in the community to the idea of the poet, half pure spirit, half biting satirist. But the latter excuse was beginning to wear thin; Cronin had not published a book of poems since his flamboyant post-university days.

'That reminds me,' said O'Shea, 'did you see Clohessy in the paper?'

Cronin's gesture combined dismissal and disgust. 'That smooth bastard!'

'He seems to be getting on,' said O'Shea carefully.

For a split second Cronin's lethargic eyes ignited with hatred.

'*On!*' he growled. 'Of course he's getting on. Hasn't he got what you need to get on in this country?'

'You mean energy?'

'I mean neck; pure, unadulterated, armour-plated, insensitive *neck*. The countryman's recipe for all occasions.'

O'Shea forbore from pointing out that like himself Cronin had been born in the country: having taken root in Dublin during his student days, he now saw himself as a city father, defending civilisation against the barbarian.

'Still, he's a fine-looking fellow,' he insinuated.

A snort was regarded as sufficient answer to that remark. But Cronin seemed to turn the matter over, for a few minutes later he raised his pint and looked across it at O'Shea. 'I'll tell you what's really wrong with Clohessy.'

O'Shea waited expectantly. What?'

'It was one of the boys in his office put me on to it. He said that Clohessy whipped over to him at one of their new Press Conference do's and took the glass from his hand telling him he had had enough.'

'Well?'

'It's the old De Valera trick brought up to date: no one ever saw that sacerdotal heron under the influence. There is something fundamentally wrong with someone who has never been seen drunk. *They can't be trusted.*'

5.15 p.m.

South of the Liffey, on a late autumn evening. People are beginning to pour from offices, Government Buildings in Kildare and Upper Merrion Street, The Tourist Board along the canal, the Electricity Supply Board on Lower Fitzwilliam Street. The stone fronts of the Georgian houses look mournful, with bulbs already lit in ground floor and basement rooms. Above the shiny, wet rows of parked cars a light mist is gathering on the trees; a plume of smoke shows where leaves are being burned in a black-railed square. At the end of a wide street rises a blue shoulder of the Dublin Mountains . . .

The curious thing, O'Shea reflected, as he swung his Volkswagen along the canal leading towards the main Cork-Limerick road, was that he actually knew Clohessy. Or rather he had known him briefly years ago, when they were both students. But why had he never mentioned the incident to anyone, not even to Cronin or Brennan? Especially when it would have been ideal material for pub gossip!

It had been a seaside resort in Donegal where O'Shea was in the habit of going for his holidays. Generally he went with a gang from the University who, to save money, camped in a field overlooking the bay. For a fortnight they racketed through the town, drinking, dancing, swimming. One year Clohessy had joined them for a few days, brought by one of O'Shea's friends. Although he moved in different circles from the rest at college (he was a member of the fencing team and secretary of something new called the Political Society), he seemed a decent enough chap, fresh-faced, rather silent. When they splashed in the diving pool or chased girls in the smoky dance hall, he tagged along though somehow a little distant and separate.

Then, one evening, a group of them were sitting out on the cliffs. The air was cool, and they felt full of youthful idealism and sadness, watching the sun go down on the Atlantic. They were discussing what they would be after they left the University. One had said he just wanted to be a good doctor, if he could get a practice. Carmody, O'Shea's bosom pal, had said (his arm looped around a girl as usual) that he wanted to see a bit of the world first: poor bastard, he had joined the Air Force and been shot down in a dog-fight over Benghazi. Another wanted to go back to teach in his home town in Tipperary. Then someone asked Clohessy what he wanted. He did not answer immediately and O'Shea remembered watching the fishing fleet sail slowly back towards the harbour. They seemed so frail and motionless and yet they kept edging imperceptibly towards their goal.

Then, in clear and precise tones, Clohessy outlined for them the shape he wished his career to follow. By twenty, he hoped to graduate with First Class Honours in Legal and Political Science; he would then enter a well-known Dublin firm as a Junior executive. By twenty-two, he would be Fencing Champion of Ireland, but would give it up afterwards: it took too much time. By twenty-five, he should be Assistant Manager and have his Doctorate in Economics. By thirty, he would certainly be a section head, but since he could hardly hope to rise any further in Ireland for the moment, he would probably go abroad and work for one of the big economic organisations, to gain top managerial experience. It was difficult to get a proper salary in Ireland at that level, but he felt sure that the government would ask him back before he was forty, to take charge of a national or semi-state organisation. Perhaps they would even create a new one, some mansized job commensurate with his training and abilities.

O'Shea heard Carmody suck in his breath sharply, whether in astonishment or in anger he did not know. The others seemed struck numb: coming from farms and country pubs, they had probably never heard anyone reveal such ambition before. Perhaps it was meant to be a joke? Clohessy, unaware of the effect he had made, was squatting like a Buddha on the esparto grass, throwing pebbles over the edge. They could hear them fall from ledge to ledge, before striking the pool at the base of the cliff. It was getting cold: one of the girls suggested they should be going in. As they left, O'Shea saw that the others avoided Clohessy.

That scene had remained in O'Shea's mind ever since, a secret source of contemptuous amazement as, year by year, he saw Clohessy's career trace the rising arc of its fulfilment, less like a human than some natural phenomenon. Would the great man remember their earlier meeting? He doubted it: he was hardly the type to bother with those who had not kept pace with him in the world. Nor was O'Shea the sort to remind him. Catching sight of the flat spaces of the Curragh, he accelerated: he still had a good distance to travel before Carricklone.

9.50 p.m.

It was the brandy and Irish coffee stage; wreaths of cigar smoke drifted slowly upwards in the dining-room of the Royal Arms Hotel, Carricklone. In the foreground, balloon glasses caught and reflected light: in the background waiters were grouped in stylish impassivity. His Lordship the Bishop of Carricklone was speaking and he was well known to detest interruption. A small man, with bushy eyebrows incongruously grafted on an old woman's face, he was launched onto one of his favourite subjects — the impurity of modern life. It had nothing to do with the problems of local development but, somehow, it always seemed to crop up in His Lordship's speeches. His pectoral cross danced as he thundered into the home stretch of his peroration.

'Gentleman, we must never betray this pearl! In this modern world of drinks and dance halls, of so-called progress and speed, our country should remain a solitary oasis. On all sides we are wooed by the sirens of lax living, but — remember this — if Ireland holds a special place in God's plan it will be due to the purity of her men and the modesty of her women.'

The bishop blew his nose with a large white handkerchief and sat down abruptly. As polite applause rippled down the table, John O'Shea looked at the faces of his companions for any response to this stirring call to arms. A dozen well fed (Galway Oysters, Roast Kerry Lamb, Carrageen Moss) and well wined (Chateauneuf Saint Patrice) faces reflected nothing but sensuous contentment. At least it was an audience of adults: the last time His Lordship had spoken it was to warn a

Confirmation class in a remote Kerry parish against the dangers of Communism.

As O'Shea's gaze reached the end of the table, it encountered the smooth full moon of Clohessy's face, sailing above an immaculate shirt front. Why did so many public figures come to look like that, as though moulded in wax? To O'Shea's surprise the left eyebrow appeared to flicker slightly in his direction, in a kind of conspiratorial schoolboy's wink. But before he could decide whether he was mistaken or not, a brandy glass rang, and he saw that Clohessy was getting to his feet to reply to the Bishop.

The voice was clear, but it took some time before O'Shea grasped the substance of the argument. It was not a dramatic speech, compared to the Bishop's, but it seemed an unobjectionable one, its points neatly tied together every now and then by a mild joke. What His Lordship had said showed his deep concern for the community, a concern they all echoed. There was often a bleakness about village life in Ireland due, not of course to our own faults, but to our sad history. The absence of trees and adjoining woods, the fact that the church was generally towards the outside of the town, the grimness of the public houses — all this made for a certain gloom. He did not mean to say that Carricklone was not a wonderful place, all Munster knew it was (this reference to the Hurling Championship brought cheers) but its charm was a trifle obscured by decayed houses and concrete run-ups. He looked forward to the day when the people of Carricklone would have the model town they obviously deserved. It was a pity that the factory that was coming was a foreign one, but we were a little retarded in these matters, and besides it would restore Carricklone's ancient links with the Continent! After that, there should be a crafts and recreation centre: it was important, as the Bishop had said, to train the young for their place in

modern life. And for the summer, a swimming pool, so that
they could meet in the open air. These new buildings could
form the nucleus of a true community; before long the people
of Carricklone might be strolling around their piazza or village square in the evenings, while from the open door of every
pub came the sound of colourful music and dancing warm as
Italy or Spain, our fellow Catholic countries.

As Clohessy sat down, to a thunder of applause, O'Shea
turned to look at the other end of the table. Most of what Clohessy said, it had slowly dawned on him, was an inversion of
the Bishop's speech, using its emotional power as a spring-
board. On paper, it would have seemed the usual parade of
clichés, but in its context, it was almost revolutionary; yet to
O'Shea's surprise, His Lordship the Bishop of Carricklone
was not merely smiling broadly, he was leading the applause.

After Clohessy, nearly everyone spoke. The Mayor of
Carricklone promised his warm support for every worthwhile
endeavour. Several local merchants pledged not merely moral
but financial assistance. The local architect and town clerk
began to compare sites for the crafts and recreation centre. As
the speeches gradually crumbled into specific discussion people changed places to keep up with them. In this excited buzz
of proposal and counter-proposal the bland mask seemed to
have settled again over Clohessy's face. He was sitting between the Lord Mayor and the Bishop's Secretary, and the
inclined head of the priest, redolent of discreet satisfaction, the
way Clohessy curled his finger round his glass or raised his
head briefly to smell his cigar before leaning confidentially
towards his companions, seemed a paradigm of worldliness.

And then the dinner was breaking up, people rising and
moving towards the door in little groups. O'Shea saw that,
with the swiftness of long training, Clohessy had already
shaken off the Lord Mayor and the Bishop's Secretary. Now

he was cruising across the room, shaking hands as he went. Having worked his way almost to the door, he came level with O'Shea, who was still standing awkwardly behind his chair. There was an instant's delay, and then his face creased into its famous smile:

'John O'Shea!' he said. 'After all these years.'

11 p.m.

'Well, what did you think of the speeches?' asked Clohessy. He and O'Shea were sitting together in the comfortable, club-like atmosphere of the hotel lounge, with the two cognacs that Clohessy had ordered before them.

'Do you mean yours of the Bishop's?' asked O'Shea carefully. Clohessy burst out laughing. 'Wasn't he wonderful! John of Carricklone is one of the last of the Old Guard: he ought to be in a museum. I heard him give the same speech two years ago in Mullingar; only there it was a sermon. I suppose,' his face became suddenly serious, 'he believes it's expected of him.'

'What do you mean?' demanded O'Shea. He was not used to this class of talk about bishops: satire, yes, he could appreciate, but friendly familiarity was a rather unsettling note.

'It's one of the troubles of being a public figure. What is the average bishop but an elderly man closed up in a palace, surrounded by people who tell him what he wants to know. Which he then tells back to them; there is nothing more corrupting than a captive audience.'

He spoke with some passion and O'Shea could not resist a probe.'

'Is that how you feel?' he inserted quietly.

Clohessy started slightly and gave O'Shea a cautious sidelong glance. But, though repenting of his outburst, he seemed willing to continue.

'Yes, a bit,' he admitted. 'But of course it's different for us.' The 'us' was so unconsciously patronising that O'Shea stung back before realising it.

'You don't mean to say you don't like it?' he said with heavy sarcasm.

'Like what?' demanded Clohessy.

'You know — the fuss, the dinners, the photographs — what people call fame. Surely —'

Clohessy gave a controlled sigh. 'Oh yes, I know what people think: that I do all this for personal gain and glory. Clohessy the big-time executive, his right hand greeting a bishop, while his left robs the nation's till. And I know I do fairly well out of it, but I regard that as a reward —'

'Reward for what?' O'Shea burst out involuntarily. Then, catching himself in time: 'What do you mean, sir?'

'You know bloody well what I mean. It's not the board meetings that kill. It's going from cocktail party to cocktail party every evening; eating chicken and ham at public banquets three times a week; never once getting angry or dropping a wrong word. How much stamina do you think that takes?'

There was such a note of sincerity, almost of agony in his voice that O'Shea was embarrassed into silence.

'And that's not the worst. Going down the country to try and put across the merit of some project — the county councillors — you saw, Christ, man, it's like being thrown to wild animals.'

'So you mean to say you don't enjoy it!' repeated O'Shea incredulously.

'Enjoy it! There's nothing I loathe more. Nowhere else in the world is a top executive at the mercy of every self important little fart with a grievance.'

'Then, why do you do it?'

Clohessy revolved the brandy glass slowly between his podgy, well-manicured hands.

'I suppose you'd call it patriotism,' he said, with some sadness.

'Patriotism!'

'Look, Sean.' At the lapse into the vernacular, O'Shea felt his spine stiffen, but Clohessy was only leaning forward with confidential eagerness.

'When I came back to this country after the war, I saw that it had no future. My first instinct was to clear out again, and to hell with it: with my background and training I could have a comfortable life anywhere in the world. You'll admit that . . .'

O'Shea nodded. There was no denying that just as some men bore the marks of sanctity, so Clohessy had the credentials for worldly success stamped on his brow.

'Then I thought that was a bit cowardly. Why not come back and try and create a future for the country at the same time as I was creating my own? As you know, we've had a lot of patriots.'

'You can say that again,' said O'Shea fervently.

'But what it has never had are a group of practical, hard-headed people who would try to put it back on its feet, like any business. People not afraid to face the priests, the politicians, the whole vast bog of the Irish middle-class, and woo something positive out of it. One would have to give up a lot, of course . . .'

'Like what?'

'Oh,' said Clohessy expansively, waving his hand in the air, 'it's not easy to define; the fleshpots of high commerce — the knighthood, the Tour d'Argent and Claridge's, the yacht at Cannes. The mistresses, even, if you like. A salesman of silk stockings could do better. The really big stuff never comes to Ireland. I know: I've seen it.'

O'Shea was silent.

'But there would be the satisfaction of being one of the first in a new line of well-trained — eh —'

'Patriots,' finished O'Shea.

'Yes.'

There was the awkwardness which often follows an unexpected burst of intimacy: the two men sat side by side, without speaking, in the curved leather armchairs. O'Shea glanced covertly once or twice at his companion, but now that urgency had left it, his face had resumed its usual bland, immobile expression. The skull was full and round, with a light fringe of silver hair on the edge of the Roman brow. The cheeks, in particular, were smooth and ruddy as though he had only been born that morning. Ten thousand mornings of close shaving, and Yardley's Lotion, had left the skin as polished as wood; even the wrinkles seemed deliberate, the necessary fine grain of maturity. It only required a Papal Cross or the panoply of an honorary degree to complete the picture of what Cronin had once called 'His Royal Emptiness'. Could such a man be sincere?

'Do you see Cronin much now?' asked Clohessy suddenly, as though divining O'Shea's thoughts.

'Now and again.'

'God, poor Cronin! The original Stone-Age Bohemian; in any other country he would have been remaindered years ago. I wouldn't mind if he did his own work, but as it is, he just mucks up both jobs. And to think that we all admired him so much at college! The pity is . . .' (thoughtfully).

'What?' asked O'Shea with some wariness.

'We could still use a man like that. Business has broadened, you know, become more intellectual, more of a science.'

'He would probably think Public Relations corrupting,' said O'Shea feebly.

Clohessy's nostrils flared. 'I hate irresponsibility like that! People like Cronin think they are the salt of the country, but what did they ever do for it? This is not Dark Rosaleen, the Silk of the Kine, but a little country trying to make its way in the world: why can't Cronin get down and push like the rest of us?'

There was an answer to that, but O'Shea couldn't think of it at the moment. Instead he finally asked the question that had been bothering him all night.

'Tell me, sir, why did you tell me all this?'

There was a pause during which O'Shea was made to feel his tactlessness. Then Clohessy rose to his feet, buttoning his short coat briskly.

'Well, you know,' he said slowly, 'there aren't really very many people one can talk to. And we are old school chums, in a manner of speaking. Besides' — O'Shea had never encountered a glance which combined affability and threat in such proportions before — 'we'll soon be working together, and I felt we should have a little talk first; on neutral ground.'

After Clohessy had gone (his chauffeur stepping smartly from the corner of the bar, where he had been waiting over a bottle of stout, to open the door for him), O'Shea remained sitting for several minutes. What Clohessy told him differed very little from what he remembered of their boyhood meeting, except for the note of idealism. Was the latter only an afterthought, to disguise the thrust of naked ambition? The fact that their talk had been planned, not spontaneous, argued as much, but he couldn't be sure. For the first time, O'Shea realised why he had never retold that original encounter: despite his surface scorn, he had never really made his mind up about Clohessy. Now he would have to make it up pretty soon.

9.50 a.m.

'Can he not wait?' asked O'Shea fretfully.

The hysteria in Nan Connor's voice came through the intercom as a sort of flat shriek. 'He just won't. He says he must speak to you. And he's beginning to use bad language.'

O'Shea looked despairingly at the litter of papers on his desk. 'All right, put him through.'

There was a crackle, a silence and then he heard Tadgh Cronin's voice intoning angrily: *'Will you for Christ's sake put me through to John O'Shea or I'll —'*

'O'Shea here.'

'Jesus, John, is that you, at last, I had a hell of a job trying to get past that female full-back you call your secretary.'

O'Shea was going to remark that after all she was only doing her duty, but all he said was: 'Well, what's on your mind?'

'I'm going to resign.'

'You're what?'

'I'm going to resign. Old Brennan told me yesterday afternoon that the Secretary had informed him that my behaviour was a disgrace to the Department and that if I didn't pull my socks up drastic action would have to be taken. Very well, says I, if it's a case of pushing or being pushed, I know my position. I'll resign!'

There was a dramatic pause, but before O'Shea could venture a comment, Cronin was away again.

'Of course, I told Brennan that it wasn't his fault, he isn't a bad old bugger. But do you know what they introduced last week: *all latecomers to sign the book in the boss's room.* No man with any pride could stand for that class of nonsense. Next thing they'll be having management classes during the tea break. Still, old Brennan looked surprised: you shoulda seen his gob drop.'

'I'll bet he was,' muttered O'Shea fervently. He would have said more, but there was a peculiar note in his friend's voice, a kind of forced complacency that warned him.

'Well, there you are, I showed them. I'd have told you last night but I couldn't find you. Where were you, by the way?'

'In Carricklone. With Clohessy,' he could not help adding.

'With Clohessy!'

Gratified by Cronin's surprise, O'Shea found himself, almost without thinking, giving an account of the previous night. At first he only described the dinner and Clohessy's speech but as he warmed up to his subject, he could not help including a (discreetly garbled) version of their interview as well. It was partly that he wanted to speak of it, partly also because he could not resist rubbing in that he had news of his own.

'You don't mean to say you swallowed that?' said Cronin incredulously.

'I don't know,' said O'Shea uneasily. 'What do you think?'

There was a pause at the other end of the line and then Cronin's voice came through, triumphant, low, almost a snarl.

'I was fucking well right!'

'What do you mean right?'

'To resign. The hour has come. *The bastards are on the march.*'

'What?'

'Listen.' O'Shea could nearly see Cronin grasping the receiver at the other end, in his excitement. 'Since this country was founded we've had two waves of chancers. The first were easy to spot; the gunmen turned gombeen: they were so ignorant that they practically ruined themselves. But this second lot are a tougher proposition. In fifty years they'll have made this country just like every place else.'

'And what's so wrong with that?'

'You know damn well what's wrong with that: they'll murder us with activity! Factories owned by Germans, posh hotels catering to the international set, computers instead of dacent pen-pushers, a typists pool: do you call that progress? Well, by Jesus, I don't, and I'll fight it tooth and nail. If this country becomes a chancer's paradise, it will be over my dead body. *Over my dead body, do you hear?'*

And that (repeated several times with increasing vehemence) was Cronin's parting shot. After vaguely agreeing to meet him for lunch in the Anchor sometime during the week, John O'Shea put down the phone, and turned to pick up the uppermost of his files. But he found it hard to concentrate, Cronin's words ringing in his ears. They had been friends for years, drawing an odd comfort from their differences of temperament, but of late O'Shea had begun to feel the strain. It was all right for Cronin to feel so defiantly about things; if the rhythm of drinking had not already corroded his faculties, his resignation might be the spur his talent needed. But for people like himself, there was no real escape: the most they could hope to find was someone under whose direction they might give of their best. Besides, was it such a criminal thing to wish to lead an ordinary life?

Somewhere, on the banks of the Liffey, or overlooking a Georgian square, a great new building would rise, a glass house against which the world might, at first, throw stones, but would gradually accept. Inside, in a large, discreetly lighted room, with Tintawn carpeting and an abstract on the wall, would be Clohessy. And in one of the adjoining cubicles, perhaps a file open before him, just as it was now. . . . Half-surprised, as though looking into a mirror, John O'Shea greeted his own future.

A Ball of Fire

IT WAS on All Souls' Day that Michael Gorman first saw the old man. He was coming back along the canal towpath. It was a walk that he liked, particularly in winter when everything emphasised the process of disintegration. The canal had not been cleaned for years, and all kind of oddments came sailing slowly by, hingeless buckets, dead animals, a skeletal pram. On the far bank there was a disused barge which sank lower into the mud each year: was it an illusion, or did its greening planks sag visibly as he watched? He halted under the dripping trees to inhale the viscous odour of a Dublin winter twilight.

It was then that the man appeared. At first he was only a shape, a vague sensation of someone at the far end of the towpath. Then it came closer and closer, a growing point on the rim of his consciousness, an affirmation of movement against the heavy stillness. As he turned to continue his walk, the figure came almost abreast. It was a small man, about five foot high, wearing a cloth cap, pulled low, and an open necked shirt. He was moving so fast that his boots drummed on the hard clay of the path. He passed Michael Gorman without a look, striking him with his shoulder so that he nearly pushed him into the water. 'Where in blazes do you think you're going,' the latter called angrily. But the little man was already half-way down towards the bridge. Above his dwindling figure, as at the end of a tunnel, the setting sun tried to burn its way through the fog, which was gradually smothering it.

He told his wife about it later that evening. She was sitting at the fire sewing a pillowcase, and he was reading aloud extracts from the evening papers. The Government was sending an Aberdeen-Angus bull to the Pope. A gang of thieves who had been terrorising the Northside were caught when they stopped to drink a case of stout in a kitchen. There was also a warm correspondence as to whether fathers should chastise their teenage daughters when they came home late. RESPONSIBLE PARENT urged the use of a supple leather strap but he was outdone by SERIOUS LASS who suggested that delinquent fathers should be beaten by their daughters. Not for the first time Michael Gorman noticed how strange his world was becoming: were there really so many sadists in Kimmage?

'That reminds me,' he said. 'I met a funny little man today. No, *met's* not the word — bumped into.'

'I know.'

'What do you mean, you know?' Her calm authority often irritated him. 'You weren't there.'

'I know because it's probably our next door neighbour.'

Three months before, it seemed, the small man had turned up next door and asked to rent the basement flat. The two old Protestant ladies who owned the house — living on the second floor in a surrealist confusion of faded draperies, ironwork and old furniture, the debris of their country home — had not seen him as a threat either to their virtue or their money, their two rival pre-occupations. Nor, since they rarely went out themselves, were they troubled by his habits, spending all day in his room, to emerge at dusk and speed like a bullet to the nearest pub. Beyond the elementary needs of shopping, he spoke to no one in the area, though once when Deirdre Gorman was coming home she had found him fumbling drunkenly at his door, and opened it for him. Whereupon he had said, with sudden distinctness: 'Thank you,' and lifted his cap.

'I think he's had a hard life,' she said contentedly.

'What do you mean?' he jeered.

'One doesn't avoid people without some good reason. He feels betrayed; I imagine he must have had an unsuccessful marriage or something like that.'

'What you mean is that if he had married someone understanding like you he might have done better, I suppose. Christ, what sentimentality! As a matter of fact, we don't even know if he was married: all we know is that he is a bloody crank.'

Deirdre Gorman laid down her sewing for a moment, and transfixed her husband with a calm blue eye. 'Why I do believe you're jealous. Of a little old man!'

It was, oddly enough, true; though he couldn't admit it. There was only one thing to do: drop the subject. Letting the papers slide to the floor in a heap, he rose to go to his studio in the adjoining room.

Michael Gorman never went willingly to his studio: he always wanted for something to give him impetus, a kick from outside. He had got a prize for drawing in the Intermediate, and vaguely thought of going to art school; but it hadn't worked out, and he soon forgot about the whole business. A decade later the impetus returned, but in a rather different form. He found himself making compulsively elaborate doodles in the office, and to safeguard his job began to draw a little at home. But even that did not satisfy his curiosity, and he started to paint, crudely at first but then (it was amazing how quickly one learned to use oils) with a bit more polish. A handful of these appeared in a local exhibition and, almost against his will, he found himself regarded as a promising young painter.

And expected to produce more when he was not even sure why he had done the first. For the second evening that week he found himself contemplating the meaningless white square of

the canvas with something like hatred. Even the smell of the
paints (and the brushes snugly reposing in their jam jar) nau-
seated him. Besides, some of them, like white lead and prus-
sian blue, were actually poisonous. Picking up a brush, he
smeared it in the palette he had just prepared (delicious!) and
began to trail it along the edge of the canvas.

What appeared at first was a kind of rough sketch of the
canal, a streak of water and low sky: he could almost smell the
rotting leaves. But with a rapidity that frightened him this
faint likeness began to submerge under a series of dark,
slashing brush-strokes. Once again, something was happening;
and he found himself fighting to keep the flow, but control it,
make it run between invisible banks like a river in spate.
Within an hour the canvas was covered with sticky, messy,
almost intractable paint, a maelstrom of pitchy colour into
which he plunged deeper and deeper. He was so exhausted that
he felt like slipping to the ground; with a last, accusing look at
the picture (what under heaven was this?) he reeled off to bed.

In the following weeks Michael Gorman saw the little man
quite frequently, like a feature of the landscape one has overlooked, which then becomes obtrusive. As he came home from
work in the evenings he would meet him scudding through the
dusk, a small parcel — loaves, eggs, a pot of jam? — under
his arm. If he went out with his wife for a walk before going
to bed they were sure to cross him lurching home from the
pub. No matter how drunk he was he always made a clutching
gesture with his cap towards Mrs Gorman, a token of respect
which clearly did not include her husband.

'I told you he was sweet,' she remarked serenely.

'Like Prussic acid, I suppose.'

'Bogman!' she smiled, moving away.

But the worst was when he appeared in The Eagle's Nest,
the pub which Michael Gorman frequented. Not that he drank

as much as he used to: the double needs of his office and studio kept him pretty well drained of surplus energy. But when a painting wasn't going well he would call on a sculptor friend of his who lived across the bridge, and accompany him for a few jars. Sometimes his wife came, but more generally not; she had never got used to the peculiar rhythm, the alternations of sluggishness and vitality, of public house drinking.

He was in the act of downing his third pint one late November evening when he saw the little man. At first he thought he was mistaken (Christ, the bastard couldn't be following him!) but sure enough, there he was, standing on his own at the end of the bar, his cap so low that it seemed part of the pint glass before him. He was going to go over and speak to him, but thought better of it, turning to the barman instead.

'Do you know who that scruffy leprechaun is at the end of the bar? The one gathered up into a ball, by himself.'

It took a minute or so, before the barman finally understood whom he meant.

'Oh, that,' he said, with relief. 'That's Mr Daly. He comes in quite often.'

'Do you think I could offer him a drink?'

The barman wiped the counter around Gorman's glass before answering.

'Well, now,' he said, 'the way it is, I wouldn't be too sure. He's a very quiet class of a man (a mechanic of some kind, I believe) and I don't think he likes to be disturbed. Do you know, like?' Whether Gorman knew or not he had to accept. What kind of protection society was there forming around this pocket misanthrope? At least, he wasn't going to be part of it; turning to his sculptor friend he announced abruptly that he was clearing home.

December came, and the weather changed, drenching the city in pale sheets of rain. His dealer had asked him for a further batch of paintings for a group exhibition, so Michael Gorman spent most of his evenings in his studio, touching up his more recent works and trying to choose between them.

That was the hardest task. He had them arranged, in varying lights, around the walls, and kept trying to come back on them quickly, as though he were a stranger. Certain pleased him immediately because of their increasing technical skill; there was an elementary artisan's pride in doing difficult, tricky things. But when he returned to them later, they looked oddly empty, despite their attractive surface: the eye rebounded from them, soothed but unsatisfied. Surely paint was only a thing to be used, like a pen or knife and fork, not an end in itself?

There were others in which there was a kind of movement, a threatening darkness, but it was so undefined as to be almost mawkish. Surely people would laugh at him if he presented things that he could not explain, or justify, even to himself? Among them was the painting he had begun over a month ago, on 1st November, and to which he had never been able to come back. Not merely did he not understand it, but it made him slightly sick to look at; so he finally turned its face to the wall.

During all that time he had nearly forgotten about his troublesome neighbour. Now and again he heard noises next door, a clanking sound, as though an old washing machine was being turned. And one night he could have sworn he heard a lorry drawing up, but in order to be sure he would have had to tiptoe through the front bedroom and pull back the blind, and he did not want to give the old man the satisfaction of spotting him. Perhaps he was moving? That would be a blessing.

Dublin at Christmas! You could sing that, Michael Gorman felt, if you had an air to it. Half-way through the month came the first party, a muffled drum-tap presaging dissolution. Then the rhythm quickened. The only real obstacle to party-going is distance; in a city of moderate size the same cast could be indefinitely reshuffled. Night and day the Gorman's phone kept ringing with invitations.

After an initial stand for sanity, Michael gave in. Instead of working in the evening, he found himself bolting a meal when he came home, and changing his clothes, before going to some party. He even began to convince himself he liked it when he found himself driving back at three in the morning for the third time in succession; and then waking to the retching consciousness of another workday dawn. He also found himself slipping out of the office during the day, to replenish the alcohol in his bloodstream.

It was on one of these outings that he absentmindedly made his way back to The Eagle's Nest. He entered through the long dark passage-way at the back to discover that, at four o'clock in the afternoon, it was as full as on a Saturday night. It was foggy, the lights had already been switched on, and there in a far corner, he spied his neighbour, Mr Daly.

This time he did not wait to ask the barman's advice. The little man's whole attitude, the silence which he spread around where he was mournfully sucking his pint, was an insult to the convivial spirit with which Michael Gorman felt himself imbued. Taking his drink in his hand he went over, and tapped him aggressively on the shoulder.

'Will you have a pint?' he said thickly.

Mr Daly did not seem to hear, so Gorman leaned his face down.

'I said will you have a drink with me,' he bellowed.

As Daly raised his head, Michael Gorman saw his face clearly for the first time. He had a pale, but neat forehead, deeply indented with lines and so thin that the bones stood out clearly under the skin. And his mouth and eyes were mild; not fearful, but curiously passive.

'Of course I'll have a drink with you,' he said clearly. 'As long as you don't shout.'

When Michael Gorman brought back the two drinks from the counter, the little man had cleared a space for him. But though he thanked him politely for the drink, he showed little inclination to talk any further. And to his surprise Michael Gorman found himself falling in with the faint melancholy of his companion's mood. Only when he was preparing to go back to the office did Daly speak to him again.

'Give my respects to your wife.'

'I will.'

'You know,' said the little man hesitantly, 'you're lucky. You have a very good woman.'

Generally Michael Gorman managed to find a brickbat buried in this remark, but this time he let it pass.

'And you own wife, sir: how is she?'

The old man looked steadily at his glass. 'Boy,' he said reminiscently, 'she was a stinger!'

The climax of the season was the party on Christmas Eve. It was held in a florid Victorian barn of a house belonging to a merchant prince who collected paintings and liked to surround himself with artists. At first Michael Gorman objected to going, on the grounds that it would be chilly, boring affair but he swiftly found out that his host had a simple recipe for a party: pour drink and music over the assembly until their faculties disintegrate. Even ten days before the result would have horrified him: now he found himself greeting the familiar uproar with quickened pulse.

As distance is measured in relation to one chosen point, so Michael Gorman determined to measure the progress of the party by observing the behaviour of the principal guest. He was an Irish writer just back from lecturing in Upsala, and for some reason he wore a deerstalker hat, in which three artificial flies were impaled. A Bloody Butcher, A Tup's Indispensable, and A Connemara Black. He looked like Christian Dior's idea of a countryman, and as Michael passed he heard a single stentorian phrase rise and float away: 'When I knew Yeats. ...'

It will be a long time till that bastard is drunk, he thought grimly. Three hours later, however, as he descended the stairs (negotiating with elaborate tact the corner where a Harvard student was trying to pinion his wife) he saw the writer slumped against the wall. His eyes were nearly closed, but he clutched Michael in an effort to convey some message.

'Plaster,' he seemed to say.

'The wall, you mean? Yes, it is pretty well done,' said Michael. The writer shook his head angrily. 'Plastered,' he said with an effort.

'Oh, you mean you're drunk,' said Michael. 'Never mind: we aren't far behind you.'

Straightening up, his companion managed to shaft his bow for the last time. *'Bastards,'* he said, and in case there should be any mistake: *'Those who have money.'*

With a rush of fellow-feeling Michael assisted him to a nearby sofa, where he fell asleep with his head on a pile of coats. Then he went to claim his wife: it was time to be going home.

As they drove down the mountainside in the early morning, Michael Gorman sang softly to himself. Although he had drunk a lot he was in one of those rare moods when drink brings an intense clarity, and the thin, pure dawn on the moors (more like water than light) invaded his mind gently. Now and again he cast an affectionate glance down to where his wife lay curled up, her head nudging his side.

When he had been a young man, tackling the Chinese Wall of chastity of the average Irish maiden, he had thought vitality the supreme virtue. He had dreamt that love, when it appeared, would be a wild flame. In his late twenties, when sexual success became easier, he had discovered to his surprise that vitality was a deceptive and dangerous thing. Now and again his relationship with his wife blazed with passion of their first meeting, but its basis lay elsewhere, in the persistent tenderness, not spasmodic but continuous, which flooded every aspect of their lives like a calm wave.

As though she felt he had been thinking of her, Deirdre Gorman straightened up. After yawning a few times, she pressed her nose against the window-pane.

'Do you know what,' she said.

'What?'

'I've been thinking about it, why I feel so sympathetic to that old man, Mr Daly I mean, our neighbour.'

'Why?'

'I think the reason is that, in some curious way, he reminds me of you. I mean, I could see you becoming like that, if everything went wrong, and there was no one to look after you.'

Michael Gorman received this news without comment: he did not feel up to digesting its implications at that hour of the morning. All he remarked was: 'Maybe we should have a look when we get back to see if he is up, and wish him a Happy Christmas.'

It was when they drew the Prefect up opposite his flat that they saw the line of milk bottles. It must have been growing on the basement ledge for days, but they had not noticed, in the confusion of party-going. After rattling down the staircase, and hammering at the door for a few minutes without answer, Michael Gorman decided to go round to the back. It probably only meant that the little man had gone away for the holidays, but it was as well to be sure.

It took him quite some time to climb laboriously over the wall separating the two gardens: in the end he had to look for a bucket to hoist his feet on. And as he let himself down on the other side, his hands scraping on the cement, he nearly stepped on a cat, which sprinted away, a thin shadow.

The walled in area at the back of the house was gloomy with neglect. A pool of rain-water had formed where the grill of a drain was clogged with dead leaves. The door was firmly locked, but there was a small barred window to the left. Raising himself with his elbow on the sill, he peered through, rubbing his sleeve against the glass. The room was dark, but he could make out some details. There was a fireplace, stuffed with old papers, which spilled into the floor. Beyond it was a filthy mattress across which — his legs dangling over the edge, his mouth open in the unseemly *rictus* of death — lay Mr Daly.

The police came an hour later, a sergeant and a chubby-faced young guard. They propped their bicycles against the railings, ceremoniously removed their clips, and clattered down the stairwell to the basement. After examining the premises, they decided that the only way to enter was by breaking down the door.

They took it in turns, moving to the back wall of the tiny courtyard, and then coming with a rush. They seemed puzzled at the resistance it offered, and after the fifth charge the young guard rubbed the thick wad of his serge uniform.

''Tis a killer, that one,' he said, as though he had been breaking down doors all his life.

Finally it gave. Not at the lock, but the centre, the whole heart of the door opening in with a rending crash as they charged one, two, in quick succession. Stepping through the splintered remains, they found why the bolts had not given way. There were four of them, one for each quarter of the door: seen from the inside it looked like a fortress.

That was the first surprise. The second came when they entered the main room. In the old days it would have been the kitchen, but now it was dark and cold, and as the light came on, a rat scampered across the blue expanse of stove which occupied the far wall. But it was not that which took them aback. Across the stone-flagged floor, orderly as a regiment on parade, stood row upon row of slot machines. Some were without handles, some had lost their symbols, some were completely disembowelled, but all were waiting, patiently in line, for the hand of the repairer.

'Jumping Jesus!' said the Sergeant.

Nor was that all. After a tour of the back rooms ('Death by natural causes, I'd say,' said the Sergeant, looking gravely down) it was decided that the young guard should remain in charge until morning. As he settled himself in with a detective story he had found in a corner, the idea occurred to him to make himself and Michael Gorman some tea. There was no gas, so he went to the meter in the hall. The shilling entered, the gas spurted; and then the coin came ringing back again, through the neat hole that had been made to facilitate its exit from the meter.

When Michael Gorman returned to his own house, instead of going immediately to bed, he went straight to his studio. Although exhausted, he felt full of a hard, flickering energy of a kind he had rarely experienced before. But as yet it was un-directed, so he prepared his paints, hoping to begin a new canvas.

And then, on impulse, he crossed the room to where his only uncompleted painting, the one of the 1st November, stood with its face to the wall. He placed it on the easel: its livid spaces stared back at him, a chaos of unfulfilment. Then he reached for a brush, and began to work.

Across the dark expanse of the canvas, a line began to develop. At first frail, like an electric wire, it grew stronger, more defined. It became a dancing, independent line, full of a weird energy, and softly radiating light. It ran right across the canvas until, completing and culminating the picture, it finished in a smothered explosion of colour, like a ball of fire.

An Occasion of Sin

ABOUT TEN miles south of Dublin, not far from Blackrock, there is a small bathing place. You turn down a side road, cross a railway bridge, and there, below the wall, is a little bay with a pier running out into the sea on the left. The water is not deep, but much calmer and warmer than at many points further along the coast. When the tide comes in, it covers the expanse of green rocks on the right, lifting the seaweed like long hair. At its highest, one can dive from the ledge of the Martello Tower, which stands partly concealed between the pier and the sea wall.

Françoise O'Meara began coming there shortly after Easter of '56. A chubby, open-faced girl, at ease with herself and the world, she had arrived from France only six months before, after her marriage. At first she hated it: the damp mists of November seemed to eat into her spirit; but she kept quiet, for her husband's sake. And when winter began to wear into spring, and the days grew softer, she felt her heart expand; it was as simple as that.

Early in the new year, her husband bought her a car, to help her pass the time when he was at the office. It was nothing much, an old Austin, with wide running boards, and rust-streaked roof, but she cleaned and polished it till it shone. With it, she explored all the little villages around Dublin: Delgany, where a pack of beagles came streaming across the road; Howth, where she wandered for hours along the cliffs; the roads above Rathfarnham. And Seacove, where she came to bathe as soon as her husband would allow her.

'But nobody bathes at this time of the year,' he said in astonishment, 'except the madmen at the Forty Foot!'

'But I *want* to!' she cried. 'What does it matter what people do. I won't melt!'

She stretched her arms wide as she spoke, and he had to admit that she didn't look as if she would; her breasts pushing her blouse, her stocky, firm hips, her wide grey eyes — he had never seen anyone look so positive in his life.

At first it was marvellous being on her own, feeling the icy shock of the water as she plunged in. It brought back a period of her childhood, spent at Etretat, on the Normandy coast: she had bathed through November, running along the deserted beach afterwards, the water drying on her body in the sharp wind. She doubted if she could do that at Seacove, but she found a corner of the wall which trapped whatever sun there was, and when the rain spat she went into the Martello Tower Café and had a bar of chocolate and a cup of tea. Sometimes it was so cold that her skin was goose-pimpled, but she loved it all; she felt she had never been so completely alive.

It was mid-May before anyone joined her along the sea wall. The earliest comer was a small fat man, who unpeeled to show a paunch carpeted with white hair. He waved to her before diving off the pierhead, and trundling straight out to sea. When he came back, his face was lobster-red with exertion, and he pummelled himself savagely with a towel. He had surprisingly small, almost dainty feet, she noticed, as he danced up and down on the stones, blowing a white column of breath into the air. As he left, he always gave her a friendly wink or called (his words swallowed by the wind): 'That beats Banagher!'

She liked him a lot. She didn't feel as much at ease with the others. An English couple came down from the *Stella Maris* boarding house to eat a picnic lunch and read the *Daily*

Express. Though sitting side by side, they rarely spoke, casting mournful glances at the sky which, even at its brightest, always had a faintly threatening aspect, like a chemical solution on the point of precipitation. And more and more local men came, mainly on bicycles. They swung to a halt along the sea wall, removing the clips from their trousers, removing their togs from the carrier, and tramping purposefully down towards the sea. One of them, who looked like a clerk (lean, bespectacled, his mouth cut into his face), carried equipment for underwater fishing, goggles, flippers and spear.

What troubled her was their method of undressing: she had never seen anything like it. First they spread a paper on the ground. Upon this they squatted, slowly unpeeling their outer garments. When they were down to shirt and trousers, they took a swift look round, and then gave a kind of convulsive wriggle, so that the lower half of the trousers hung limply. There was a brief glimpse of white before a towel was wrapped across the loins; gradually the full length of the trousers unwound, in a series of convulsive shudders. A further lunge and the togs went sliding up the thighs, until they struck the outcrop of the hipbone. A second look round, a swift pull of the towel with the left hand, a jerk of the togs with the right, and the job was done. Or nearly: creaking to their feet, they pulled their thigh-length shirts over their heads to reveal pallid torsos.

At the beginning, this procedure amused her: it looked like a comedy sequence, especially as it had to be performed in reverse, when they came out of the water. But then it began to worry her: why were they doing it? Was it because there were women present? But there were none apart from the Englishman's wife, who sat gazing out to sea, munching her sandwiches: and herself. But she had seen men undressing on beaches ever since she was a child and hardly even noticed it.

In any case, the division of the human race into male and female was an interesting fact with which she had come to terms long ago: she did not need to have her attention called to it in such an extraordinary way.

What troubled her even more was the way they watched her when she was undressing. She usually had her togs on under her dress; when she hadn't, she sat on the edge of the sea wall, sliding the bathing suit swiftly up her body, before jumping down to pull the dress over her head: the speed and cleanness of the motion pleased her. But as she fastened the straps over her back she could feel eyes on her every move: she felt like an animal in a cage. And it was not either curiosity or admiration, because when she raised her eyes, they all looked swiftly away. The man with the goggles was the worst: she caught him gazing at her avidly, the black band pushed up around his ears, like a racing motorist. She smiled to cover her embarrassment but to her surprise, he turned his head, with an angry snap. What was wrong with her?

Because there was something: it just wasn't right, and she wanted to leave. She mentioned her doubts to her husband who laughed and then grew thoughtful.

'You're not very sympathetic,' he pointed out. 'After all, this is a cold country. People are not used to the sun.'

'Rubbish,' she replied. 'It's as warm as Normandy. It's something more than that.'

'Maybe it's just modesty.'

'Then why do they look at me like that? They're as lecherous as troopers but they won't admit it.'

'You don't understand,' he retreated.

It was mid-June when the clerical students appeared at Seacove. They came along the coast road from Dun Laoghaire on bicycles, black as a flock of crows. Their coats flapped in the sea-wind as they tried to pass each other out, rising on the pedals. They curved down the side-road towards the Martello Tower, where they piled their machines into the wooden racks, solemn-looking Raleighs and low-handled racers.

When they appeared, some of them had started undressing, taking off their coats and hard clerical collars as they came. Most already had their togs on, steeping out of their trousers on the beach, to create a huddle of identical black clothes. The others undressed in a group under the shadow of the sea wall, and then came racing down; together they trooped towards the pierhead.

For the next quarter of an hour the sea was teeming with them, dense as a shoal of mackerel. They plunged, they splashed, they turned upside down. One who was timid kept retreating to the shallow water, but two others stole up and ducked him vigorously, only to be buffeted, from behind, in their turn. The surface of the water was cut into clouds of spray. Far out the arms of the three strongest swimmers flashed, in a race to the lighthouse point.

When they came out of the sea to dry and lie down, they generally found a space cleared around their clothes, the people having withdrawn to give them more room. But the clerical students did not seem to observe, or mind, plumping themselves down in whatever space offered. One or two had brought books, but the majority lay on their backs, talking and laughing. At first their chatter disturbed Françoise from the novel she was reading, but it soon sank into her consciousness, like a litany.

'But Pius always had a great cult of the Virgin. They say he saw her in the Vatican gardens.'

'If Carlow had banged in that penalty, they'd be in the final Sunday.'

'Father Conroy says that after the second year in the bush you nearly forget home exists.'

While she was amused by their energy, Françoise would probably not have spoken to them, but for the accident of falling asleep one day, a yellow edition of Mauriac lying across her stomach. When she awoke, the students were settling around her. It was a warm day, and their usual place near the water had been taken by a group of English families with children, so they looked for the nearest free area. Although they pretended indifference, she could feel a current of curiosity running through them at finding her so close; now and again she caught a shy glance, or a chuckle, as one glanced at another meaningfully. Among their white skins and long shorts, she became suddenly conscious of her gay blue- and red-striped bathing suit, blazing like a flag in the sunshine. And of her already browning legs and arms.

'Is that French you're reading?' said one finally. Just back from a second plunge in the sea, he was towelling himself slowly, shaking drops of water over everyone. He had a coarse, friendly face, covered with blotches, and a shock of carroty hair, which stuck up in wet tufts.

She held up the volume in answer. *'Le Fleuve de Feu,'* she spelled; 'the river of fire, one of Mauriac's novels.'

'He's a Catholic writer, isn't he?' said another, with sudden interest. The other turned to look at him, and he flushed brick-red, sitting his ground.

'Well,' she grimaced, remembering certain episodes in the novel, 'he is and he isn't. He's very bleak, in an old-fashioned sort of way. The river of fire is meant to be,' she searched for the words, 'the flood of human passion.'

There was silence for a minute or two. 'Are you French?' said a wondering voice.

'Yes, I am,' she confessed, apologetically, 'but I'm married to an Irishman.'

'We thought you couldn't be from here,' said another voice, triumphantly. Everyone seemed more at ease, now that her national identity had been established. They talked idly for a few minutes, before the red-haired boy, who seemed to be in charge, looked at his watch and said it was time to go. They all dressed quickly, and as they sailed along the sea wall on their bicycles (she could only see their heads, like moving targets in a funfair) they waved to her.

'See you tomorrow,' they called gaily.

By early July the meetings between Françoise and the students had become a daily affair. As they rode up on their bicycles they would call out to her, 'Hello, Françoise.' And after they bathed, they came clambering up the rocks, to sit around her in a semi-circle. Usually the big red-haired boy (called 'Ginger' by his companions) would start the conversation with a staccato demand: 'What part of France are you from?' or, 'Do ye like it here?' but the others soon took over, while he sank back into a satisfied silence, like a dog that had performed an expected trick.

At first the conversation was general: Françoise felt like a teacher as they questioned her about life in Paris. And whatever she told them seemed to take on such an air of unreality, more like a lesson than real life. They liked to hear about the Louvre, or Notre-Dame, but when she tried to tell them of what she knew best, the student life around the Latin Quarter, their attention slid away. But it was not her fault, because when she questioned them about their own future (they were going on to the Missions), they were equally vague. It was as though only what related to the present was real, and anything else exotic; unless one was plunged into it, when, of course, it became normal. Such torpidity angered her.

'But wouldn't you like to see Paris?' she exclaimed.

They looked at each other. Yes, they would like to see Paris, and might, some day, on the way back from Africa. But what they really wanted to do was to learn French: all they got was a few lessons a week from Father Dundee.

Another day they spoke of the worker priests. Fresh from the convent, *a jeune fille bien pensante*, Françoise had plunged into social work, around the rue Belhomme and the fringes of Montmartre. And she had come to know several of the worker priests. One she knew had fallen in love with a prostitute and had to struggle to save his vocation: she thought him a wonderful man. But her story was received in silence; a world where people did not go to mass, where passion was organised and dangerous, did not exist for them, except as a textbook vision of evil.

'Things must be very lax in France,' said Ginger rising up.

She could have brained him.

Still, she enjoyed their company, and felt quite disappointed whenever (because of examinations or some religious ceremony), they did not show up. And it was not just because they fulfilled a woman's dream to find herself surrounded by admiring men. Totally at ease with her, they offered no calculation of seduction or flattery, except a kind of friendly teasing. It reminded her of when she had played with her brothers (she was the only girl) through the long summer holidays; that their relationship might not seem as innocent to others never crossed her mind.

She was lying on the sea wall after her swim, one afternoon, when she felt a shadow move across her vision. At first she thought it was one of the students, though they had told her the day before that they might not be coming. But no; it was the small fat man who had been one of the first to join her at Seacove. She smiled up at him in welcome, shielding her eyes against the sun. But he did not smile back, sitting down beside her heavily, his usual cheery face set in an attempt at solemnity.

'Missing your little friends today?'

She laughed. 'Yes, a bit,' she confessed. 'I rather like them, they're very pleasant company.'

He remained silent for a moment. 'I'm not sure it's right for you to be talking to them,' he plunged.

She sat up with a jerk. 'But what do you mean?'

'Lots of people on the beach' — he was obviously uncomfortable — 'are talking.'

'But they're only children!' Her shock was so deep that she was trembling: if such an inoffensive man believed this, what must the others be thinking?

'They're clerical students,' he said stubbornly. 'They're going to be priests.'

'But all the more reason: one can't,' she searched for the word, '*isolate* them.'

'That's not how we see it. You're giving bad example.'

'I'm giving what?'

'Bad example.'

Against her will, she felt tears prick the corners of her eyes. 'Do you believe that?' she asked, attempting to smile.

'I don't know,' he said seriously. 'It's a matter for your conscience. But it's not right for a single girl to be making free with clerical students.'

'But I'm not single!'

It was his turn to be shocked. 'You're a married woman! And you come —'

He did not end the sentence but she knew what he meant.

'Yes, I'm a married woman, and my husband lets me go to the beach on my own, and talk to whoever I like. You see, he trusts me.'

He rose slowly. 'Well, daughter,' he said, with a baffled return to kindliness, 'it's up to yourself. I only wanted to warn you.'

As he padded heavily away, she saw that the whole beach was watching her. This time she did not smile, but stared straight in front of her. There was a procession of yachts making towards Dun Laoghaire harbour, their white sails like butterflies. Turning over, she hid her face against the concrete, and began to cry.

But what was she going to do? As she drove back towards Dublin, Françoise was so absorbed that she nearly got into an accident, obeying an ancient reflex to turn on the right into the Georgian street where they lived. An oncoming Ford hooted loudly, and she swung her car up onto the pavement, just in time. She saw her husband's surprised face looking through the window: thank God he was home.

She did not mention the matter, however, until several hours later, when she was no longer as upset as she had been at the beach. And when she did come round to it, she tried to tell it as lightly as possible, hoping to distance it for herself, to see it clearly. But though her husband laughed a little at the beginning, his face became more serious, and she felt her nervousness rising again.

'But what right had he to say that to me?' she burst out, finally.

Kieran O'Meara did not answer, but kept turning the pages of the *Evening Press*.

'What right has anyone to accuse people like that?' she repeated.

'Obviously he though he was doing the right thing.'

She hesitated. 'But surely you don't think . . .'

His face became a little red, as he answered. 'No, of course not. But I don't deny that in certain circumstances you might be classed as an occasion of sin.'

She sat down with a bump in the armchair, a dishcloth in her hand. At first she felt like laughing, but after repeating the phrase 'an occasion of sin' to herself a few times, she no longer found it funny and felt like crying. Did everyone in this country measure things like this? At a party, a few nights before, one of her husband's friends had solemnly told her that 'sex was the worst sin because it was the most pleasant.' Another had gripped her arm, once, crossing the street: 'Be careful.' 'But you're in danger too!' she laughed, only to hear his answer. 'It's not myself I'm worried about, it's you. I'm in the state of sanctifying grace.' The face of the small fat man swam up before her, full of painful self-righteousness, as he told her she was 'giving bad example'. What in the name of God was she doing in this benighted place?

'Do you find me an occasion of sin?' she said, at last, in a strangled voice.

'It's different for me,' he said, impatiently. 'After all, we're married.'

It came as a complete surprise to him to see her rise from the chair, throw the dishcloth on the table, and vanish from the room. Soon he heard the front door bang, and her feet running down the steps.

Hands in the pockets of her white raincoat, Françoise O'Meara strode along the bank of the Grand Canal. There was a thin rain falling, but she ignored it, glad if anything for its damp imprint upon her face. Trees swam up to her, out of the haze: a pair of lovers were leaning against one of them, their faces blending. Neither of them had coats, they must be soaked through, but they did not seem to mind.

Well, there was a pair who were enjoying themselves, anyway. But why did they have to choose the dampest place in all Dublin, risking double pneumonia to add to their troubles? What was this instinct to seek darkness and discomfort, rather than the friendly light of day? She remembered the couples lying on the deck of the Holyhead boat when she had come over: she had to stumble over them in order to get down the stairs. It was like night-time in a bombed city, people hiding from the blows of fate; she had never had such a sense of desolation. And then, when she had negotiated the noise and porter stains of the Saloon and got to the Ladies, she found that the paper was strewn across the floor and that someone had scrawled FUCK CAVAN in lipstick on the mirror.

Her husband had nearly split his sides laughing when she asked what that meant. And yet, despite his education and travel, he was as odd as any of them. From the outside, he looked completely normal, especially when he left for the office in the morning in his neat executive's suit. But inside he was a nest of superstition and stubbornness; it was like living with a Zulu tribesman. It emerged in all kinds of small things: the way he avoided walking under ladders, the way he always blessed himself during thunderstorms, the way he saluted every church he passed, a hand flying from the wheel to his forehead even in the thick of city traffic. And that wasn't the worst. One night she had woken up to see him sitting bolt upright in bed, his face tense and white.

'Do you hear it?' he managed to say.

Faintly, on the wind, she heard a crying sound, a sort of wail. It sounded weird all right, but it was probably only some animal locked out, or in heat, the kind of thing one hears in any garden, only magnified by the echo-chamber of the night.

'It's a banshee,' he said. 'They follow our family. Aunt Margaret must be going to die.'

And, strangely enough, Aunt Margaret did die, but several weeks later, and from old age more than anything else: she was over eighty and could have toppled into the grave at any time. But all through the funeral, Kieran kept looking at Françoise reproachfully, as if to say *you see*! And now the disease was beginning to get at her, sending her to stalk through the night like a Mauriac heroine, melancholy eating at her heart. As she approached Lesson Street Bridge, she saw two swans, a cob and a pen, moving slowly down the current. Behind them, almost indistinguishable because of their grey feathers, came four young ones. The sight calmed her: it was time to go back. Though he deserved it, she did not want her husband to be worrying about her. In any case, she had more or less decided what she was going to do.

The important thing was not to show, by the least sign, that she was troubled by what they thought of her. Swinging her togs in her left hand, Françoise O'Meara sauntered down towards the beach at Seacove. It was already pretty full, but, as though by design, a little space had been left, directly under the sea wall, where she usually sat. So she was to be ostracised as well! She would show them: with a delicious sense of her audience she hoisted herself up onto the concrete and began to undress. But she was only halfway through changing when the students arrived. In an ordinary way, she would have taken this in her stride, but she saw the people watching them as they tramped over, and the clasp of her bra stuck, and she was left to greet them half in, half out of her dress. And when she did get the bathing suit straightened she saw that, since they had all arrived more or less together, they were expecting her to join them in a swim. Laying his towel out carefully on the ground, like an altar-cloth, Ginger turned towards the sea: 'Coming?'

Scarlet-faced, she marched down with him to the pierhead. The tide was high, and just below the Martello Tower the man with the goggles broke surface, spluttering, as though on purpose to stare at her. A little way out, a group of clerical students were horse-playing: she wasn't going to join in *that*. Without speaking to her companion, she struck out towards the Lighthouse Point, cutting the water with a swift sidestroke. But before she had gone far, she found Ginger at her side: and another boy on the other. Passing (they both knew the crawl), falling back, repassing, they accompanied her out to the point, and back again. Were they never to leave her alone?

And afterwards when they lay on the beach, they kept pestering her with questions. And not the usual ones, but much bolder, in an innocent sort of way: what had got into them? It was the boy who had asked about Mauriac who begin it, wanting to know if she ended the book, whether she knew any people like that, what she thought of its view of love. And then, out of the blue:

'What's it like, to be married?'

She rolled over on her stomach and looked at him. No, he was not being roguish, he was quite serious, gazing at her with interest, as were most of the others. But how could one answer such a question, before such an audience?

'Well, it's very important for a woman, naturally,' she began, feeling as ripe with clichés as a Woman's page columnist. 'And not just because people — society — imply that if a woman is not married that she's a failure: that's a terrible trap. And it is not merely living together, though —' She looked at them: they were still intent. '— that's pleasant enough, but in order to fulfil herself, in the process of giving. And that's the whole paradox, that if it's a true marriage, she feels freer, just because she has given.'

'Freer?'

'Yes, freer after marriage than before it. It's not like an affair, where though the feeling may be as intense, one knows that one can escape. The freedom in marriage is the freedom of having committed oneself: at least that's true for the woman.' Her remarks were received in silence, but it was not the puzzled silence of their first meetings, but a thoughtful one, as though, while they could not quite understand what she meant, they were prepared to examine it. But she still could not quiet a nagging doubt in her mind, and demanded: 'What made you ask me that?'

It was not her questioner, but Ginger, who had hardly been listening, who gave her her answer. 'Sure, it's well known,' he said pleasantly, gathering up his belongings, 'that French women think about nothing but love.'

He pronounced it 'luve', with a deep curl in the vowel. Before she think of a reply, they were half-way across the beach.

She was still raging when she got home, all the more so since she knew she could not tell her husband about it. She was still raging when she went to bed, shifting so much that she made her husband grunt irritably. She was still raging when she woke up, from a dream in which the experience lay curdled.

She dreamt that she was at Seacove in the early morning. The sea was a deep running green, with small waves, hitting the pierhead. There was no one in sight so she took off her clothes and slipped into the water. She was half-way across to the Lighthouse Point when she sensed something beneath her: it was the man with the goggles, his black flippers beating the water soundlessly as he surged up towards her. His eyes roved over her naked body as he reached out for her leg. She felt herself being pulled under, and kicked out strongly. She heard the glass of his goggles smash as she broke to the surface again; where her husband was drawing the blinds to let in the morning light.

Today, she decided, she must end the whole stupid affair: it had gone on too long, caused her too much worry. After all, the people who had protested were probably right: the fact that the boys were getting fresh with her proved it. She toyed with the idea of just not going back to the beach, but it seemed cowardly. Better to face the students directly, and tell them she could not see them again.

So when they arrived at the beach in the mid-afternoon they found her sitting stiffly against the sea wall, a book resting on her knees. Saluting her with their usual friendliness, they got hardly any reply. At the time, they passed no remarks, but lying on the beach after their swim they found the silence heavy and tried to coax her with questions. But she cut them short each time, ostentatiously returning to her book.

'Is there anything wrong?' one of them asked, at last.

Keeping her eyes fixed on the print, she nodded. 'More or less.'

'It wouldn't have anything to do with us?' This from Ginger, with sudden probing interest.

'As a matter of fact, it has.' Shyness slowly giving way to relief, she told about her conversation with the little fat man. 'But, of course, it's really my fault,' she ended lamely. 'I should have known better.'

Waiting their judgement, she looked up. To her surprise, they were smiling at her, affectionately.

'Is that all?'

'Isn't it enough?'

'But sure we knew all that before.'

'You know it!' she exclaimed in horror. 'But how . . .

'Somebody came to the College a few days ago and complained to the Dean.'

'He asked us what you were like.'

'And what did you say?' she breathed.

'We said' — the tone was teasing but sincere — 'we said you were a better French teacher than Father Dundee.'

The casual innocence of the remark, restoring the whole heart of their relationship, brought a shout of laughter from her. But as her surprise wore off, she could not resist picking at it, suspiciously, at least once more.

'But what about what the people said? Didn't it upset you?'

Ginger's gaze seemed to rest on her for a moment, and then moved away, bouncing like a rubber ball down the steps, towards the sea.

'Ach, sure people would see bad in anythin,' he said easily.

And that was all: no longer interested, they turned to talk about something else. They were going on their holidays soon (no wonder they were so frisky!) and wouldn't be seeing her much again. But they had enjoyed meeting her; maybe she would be there next year? She lay with her back against the sea wall, listening to them, her new book (it was Simone de Beauvoir's *Le Deuxième Sexe*) at her side. A movement caught her eye down the beach; someone was trying to climb on the to the ledge of the Martello Tower. First came the spear, then the black goggles, then the flippers, like an emerging sea monster. Remembering her dream, she began to laugh again, so much so that her companions looked at her inquiringly. Yes, she said quickly, she might be at Seacove next year.

Though in her heart she knew that she wouldn't.

Death of a Chieftain

REVOLVER IN one hand, machete in the other, his T-shirt moist with sweat (except where the raft of the sun hat kept a circle of white about his shoulders), he beat his way through the jungle around San Antonio. Behind him followed a retinue of *peons*, tangle-haired, liquid-eyed, carrying the inevitable burden of impedimenta. With their slow pace, their resigned gestures, they seemed less like human beings than like a column of ants, winding its way patiently over and a round obstacles.

When they came to a clearing that satisfied him, he declared a halt, calling up his carriers in succession. The first put down the table he had been hugging across his shoulders, peering through its front legs for the path ahead. Around the table were piled various instruments and items of food with, to top the mound, a bottle of *tequila* and a neat six-pack of Budweiser beer. With the air of an acolyte bringing a ritual to its conclusion the last carrier approached, lugging a battered cane-chair. Bernard Corunna Coote sat down, breathing heavily.

Food, first. Like a bear let loose ίn a tuckshop, he ransacked the parcels, tearing the tinfoil or polythene bags open. Half an hour later, while the natives lay around, somnolent as stones after their brief meal of *tacos*, he was still fighting his way through a cold roast chicken, washed down by draughts of lukewarm beer. Wiping his mouth, he turned to work.

Compass and sextant, lovingly consulted, pinpointed his position. Then he erected a triangular instrument, like a theodolite, and took readings, both horizontal and vertical. As though satisfied of where he stood, but not what he stood on, he produced a gleaming spade and began to sink holes around the clearing. From them he took 'samples', handfuls of red clay and stone, which he heaped on the table, to the height of a child's sandcastle.

By the time he was finished, the whole clearing looked as if it had been attacked by a regiment of moles. From under their conical hats the Indians watched: now it was their turn. Exasperated by their sleepy gaze, he dispatched runners into the forest to bring back further samples. When they returned to lay their spoils before him (curiously shaped fragments of flint, stones faintly resembling arrowheads, stones in which veins of mica flashed) he interrogated them about anything they might have seen, with an optimism that only gradually died into disappointment.

All these details were entered on a large roll-like map of the district. At the top of the chart, in a fair hand, was inscribed the Indian name of the region: *Coatlicue*, the land of the Goddess of Death. At the bottom was the owner's name: *Bernard Corunna Coote, His Property*. In between, from the central axis of San Antonio, the ever increasing lines of his excursions radiated outwards, like a spider's web.

If the centre of the spider's web was San Antonio, the centre of San Antonio, as far as Bernard Corunna Coote was concerned, was the Hotel Darien. It stood on a promontory overlooking the town, a great bathtub of a building whose peeling façade was only partly disguised by a fringe of palm trees. The disparity between its size and the adobe hovels gathered around its base would have been shocking, were it not for its enormously dilapidated appearance, like a rogue mosque. From whatever angle one approached, its grey dome was the first thing to become visible; a landmark to the market-going Indian, slumped on his burro, a surprise to the traveller, who felt as though he were arriving at Penn Station or St Pancras.

The history of the Hotel Darien combined mercantile greed with the dispairing quality of romance. In the 1890s, after the failure of the de Lesseps Panama project, a group of Liverpool and New York businessmen (already linked by the golden chain of considerable shipping profits) had been taken by the idea of cutting a railroad through the jungles of Central America. Such a railway would save ships the dangerous journey round Cape Horn: cargo could be shipped across the isthmus in a day. The tiny fishing villages at either end would become great ports, where the goods of half a continent were transferred from boat to rail and vice-versa. And so the Hotel Darien came into existence, a luxury hotel where top-hatted businessmen could relax, gazing proprietorially out onto the Pacific.

And then, in 1902, while the first cowcatcher was pushing its way through the jungle, news came that the United States had taken over the Panama Canal project. The Hotel Darien did not die immediately: one does not destroy a white elephant if it has been sufficiently expensive to construct. The railway came in due course and though the opening was less spectacular than planned (*il Presidente's* speech was drowned in a tropical thunder-storm) there was a little light traffic, especially tourists attracted by the idea of travelling through savage country, with a stout pane of glass between them and the alligators. But it degenerated into a jungle local, staggering from village to village, its opulent carriages white with bird-droppings.

Business picked up slightly in the 1920s with the planning of the Pan-American Highway. But even that passed about fifty miles away and only occasional parties deviated to San Antonio, drawn by the legend of the railway or by the few ex-

cavated archaeological remains in the area. Gradually the
Hotel Darien sank to what seemed its place in the scheme of
things, a remote limbo for remittance men, unwanted third
sons, minor criminals, all those whose need for solitude was
greater than their fear of boredom. And strays from nowhere
that anyone had ever heard of, like Bernard Corunna Coote.

Bernard Corunna Coote came to San Antonio in the late
summer of 1950, part of a guided tour from Boston. He
looked out of place from the beginning, a large man, sweating
it out in baggy flannels and tweed coat, with, perched incongruously on his forehead (like a snowcap on a tropical peak),
the remains of a cricketer's cap. He stank of drink and had the
edgy motions of someone who had not slept for days: black
circles were packed under his eyes.

His companions skirted him as they descended from the
bus. Only one person showed any interest in his arrival: from
his niche under a pillar on the shady side of the square, Hautmoc, the town drunkard, opened an opportunistic eye. When
the American matrons chattered off, armed with cameras, in
search of the colourful town market, Hautmoc moved in. He
found Bernard Corunna Coote sitting on the terrace of the
town café, drinking *tequila*.

'Señor,' he said, with sweeping politeness, 'may I join
you?'

When the main party of SUNLITE TOURS returned, Hautmoc and his companion were still deep in conversation. Originally spotted as a soft touch, something in the uneasy bulk of
his victim had moved Hautmoc, who was busily explaining to
him his favourite subject: the ethnological basis of American
civilisation. His mahogany face, mystical with drink, leaned
towards the white man.

'But in the mountains, beyond the Spaniards' reach, the poor people remained,' he oracled. 'They — we — I are still a pure race.'

Coote did not speak, but his eyes flickered interest.

'Spaniards, bah! a decadent syphilitic race from a dead continent. Mexicans, bah! a spawn of half-breeds. The true Indian . . .'

The SUNLITE TOURS bus was loading in the square. As the negro courier looked over, sounding his klaxon, his passenger ordered another *tequila*.

'You were saying?' he asked.

'The true Indian, *los hombres de la sierra*, are the aristocrats of this hemisphere, the purest people in the world.'

The courier came towards them, touching his hand to his yellow SUNLITE cap.

'Mr Coote, we're leaving now, sir.'

Bernard Corunna Coote turned up a watery, but firm, eye. 'I have just discovered the purest people in the western world,' he said in Spanish. 'In such circumstances, one does not leave. *Yo me quedo aqui.*'

As the bus roared from the square, a surprised line of New England matrons saw their late travelling companion and an unknown Indian, their two heads together, roaring with laughter. Between them, like a third party, stood the new bottle of *tequila*.

'In the old days,' said Hautmoc, with a meaningful gesture towards the bus, 'we would have sacrificed *them*. A land must be irrigated with blood!'

And thus Bernard Corunna Coote became one of the permanent guests of the Hotel Darien, and as much a feature of the town in his own way as Hautmoc. Daily he padded down to the square for a morning drink, and to collect his mail. According to the postmaster, a quiet student of these matters, most of the letters bore a king's head and came from Inglaterra. But there was also a newspaper bearing the ugliest stamps he had ever seen, a pale hand clutching a phallic sword, and surrounded by what looked like (but was not, as he found when he consulted the dictionary) Old German script. It was all mildly puzzling, and he took the unusual step of being polite to Hautmoc when he next met him, hinting at a free drink if information was forthcoming. But as everyone had long ago agreed, the latter was a cracked vessel, returning little or no sound, except his pet theories about race and human sacrifice.

'I don't know,' he said, screwing his eyes like an animal dragged into the light. '*Es muy difícil*. He says he is from the oldest civilisation in Europe, as old as the Indian. But it is not English.'

To the rest of the town he was *el Señor Doctor*, the brooding figure whose place at the café table no one ever took, even on market days. The schoolboy cap had given way to a wide-brimmed sun hat, the tweed coat had disappeared, he wore floppy cotton drawers, and rope-soled sandals instead of Oxfords, but they could still recognise a learned man when they saw one. Even if mad: catching those large, watery eyes upon them the women in the market-place drew there *rebozos* over their heads and made a gesture of expiation as they bent to ruffle among their baskets of fruit and pottery.

II

The people in a position to know most about *el Señor Doctor* were those who appeared to care least: the three other permanent guests of the Hotel Darien. The oldest was not really a guest, being the hotel manager, but he had so little work to do (and that little he tended to leave to the servants) that only rarely were his companions reminded of their business relationship with him. A cadaverous Iowan, called Mitchell Witchbourne, his bony features had the asceticism of a Grant Wood painting: one looked behind him, expecting to see a clapboard barn and silo. This impression of weathered starkness was increased by his high-pitched voice. Night and day it creaked, like a weather-vane, sending out stories, jokes, hints of what looked like hope and communication, but gradually took on the shrillness of signals of distress. At forty he had been manager of a chain of Mid-Western hotels, from Chicago to Colorado: what had brought him, ten years later, to a decaying seaport on the Pacific coast?

No one knew either what had brought Jean Tarrou, the neatly moustached little Frenchman who spoke English with a slurred brokenness which grew more charming each year. A devotee of *la culture physique*, his room was full of mechanical contraptions upon which he practised nightly. (An American matron, hearing the sounds from the adjoining room, had burst indignantly in to find him squatting in black tights on the carpet, one hand held high, the other pointing sideways, a human semaphore. His legs were caught up in pulleys, towards the ceiling, at an angle of forty-five degrees.) Now and again he dropped hints of a distinguished past, a *licence ès-lettres* from the Sorbonne, consular service in the West Indies, but the trail came to an abrupt end with the last war. He had served under Vichy, but did not detest de Gaulle, a paradox which indicated that his troubles were as much private as political. In any case, like most French people, he did not discuss matters with people outside his family circle, even when, as in San Antonio, they were either far away, or non-existent.

The person about whom most was known was Carlos Turbida, who was still young enough to derive satisfaction from the idea of being a black sheep. The son of a wealthy

Mexican fish merchant, his father had retired him from the capital after his third paternity suit (it was not the behaviour he objected to, but the carelessness). Officially, he was in charge of the south-west section of the family fishing fleet, and, once a week, he roared away in his Porsche to the nearby harbour. Tarrou had seen him there, the distinctive olive-green machine parked among the fishing nets while a bored captain pretended to listen, as he strutted up and down the quay. He even cultivated a sailor's walk, but the effect was not so much athletic as sexual: he rolled his hips as though carrying a gun. But generally he lay in bed, eating sweets, reading movie magazines, and dreaming of Acapulco: the perfect portrait of the Latin-American *cicisbeo*.

The main interest in Coote was mathematical: he made the necessary fourth for the most card games, poker, bridge, gin rummy. To endure the silence of a place like San Antonio habit was indispensable. Five evenings a week they played, grouped around a table on the veranda, while the tropical night grew heavy outside, and the Indian waiter came, bringing a lamp and fresh drinks. At first they played for *pesos*, but then, disdaining the effort of tossing coins on the baize, they turned to counters, using matchsticks as chips. As the sums involved mounted — from tens they progressed to hundreds and sometimes thousands — even that kind of tally became impossible. So each time the soberest of them (it was usually Tarrou) kept a record. Though their skills were equal, it was necessary, to keep an edge on the game, to believe in some apocalyptic day of reckoning: in the meantime, there was the drug of ritual contest, with memory floating to the surface as the hands were occupied.

'I remember once,' said Turbida, 'driving from Monterey to Mexico City. You know the road?' He raised two fingers to indicate a bid.

'Up, up, up,' said Witchbourne, sawing an imaginary steering wheel. 'Then, down, down, down.' He clutched his stomach.

'I spent the night in a little hotel, high up in the Sierra Madre. In the corridor, outside my room, I see the, how you say, chambermaid. She had long black hair, down her back, a pure Huastecan Indian. As she pass, I take hold of it.'

'I pass,' said Tarrou, and poised his pencil over the white slip of paper at his side.

'Let me go, she cries, let me go. There were tears in her eyes. I say, I let you go, if you come back to stay. That night, I sleep with her six times. She cries again when I leave in the morning. What can you do with silly girls like that?'

'You can only eat them,' said Tarrou, pleasantly.

'I'll see you, said Coote, hunching his shoulders across the table towards Turbida. The latter laid down his hand calmly: in the heart of his palm two dark queens lay, without embarrassment, beside two smiling red knaves.

'Damn,' said Coote.

There was silence while Tarrou shuffled the cards, laying them (with that pedantic precision he brought to every action) in a neat semi-circle before each man. If Turbida's stories were mainly sexual, his were more frightening, tasteful vignettes of people and places which only gradually revealed, under their smooth surface, an underlying terror.

'It is on that route, if I remember rightly,' he said, 'that the natives bring one glasses of freshly crushed orange juice. The bus stops by the groves just at midnight and the whole air is full of the smell of oranges.'

Both Witchbourne and Coote reached simultaneously for more whiskey.

'But it is not quite as gracious a custom as on the route to Vera Cruz,' he continued. 'There is a little station there, just before the railway descends from the mountains, where the women come, selling camellias laid out in hollow canes, like little coffins. It is only then that one notices that most of the women are crippled: one has no fingers, another no nose, a third a stump instead of a leg.'

'Heredo-syphilis,' said Witchbourne gruffly, 'the Spanish pox. These mountain villages, no water, no medical services, intermarriage: never get rid of it.' His moustaches were bright with whiskey.

'I bid you a hundred pesos.'

'I raise you fifty,' said Turbida excitedly.

As Coote threw in his hand, Tarrou leaned forward, delicately poised as a cat. 'I will raise you both fifty,' he stated. After a further flurry of bids, the others faltered, throwing in their hands. While Tarrou recorded his victory, Witchbourne swept up the cards for the next deal, glancing swiftly at the Frenchman's as he did so: three fours.

Of Witchbourne's conversation there was little to be said: the past for him was a devastated territory, a no-man's-land, through which he wandered, picking up fragments. Hardly anything he said could be added to anything else, the only recurrent factor being his practice of ending the evening by telling a joke. And his favourite was the story of *The Vicar and his Ass*. When he began, everyone tensed, assuming stares of interest, like executives on a board meeting.

'There was a parish in the mountains where the people had a long way to go to church. So they all went on their asses, and to pass the time, they played games, the boys pinching the girls' asses and the girls' asses biting the boys' asses. Then they tethered all the asses at the church door. One day during the revolution, a bomb fell in the graveyard. In the confusion, everyone jumped through the windows, the boys falling on the girls' asses, the girls on the boys' asses. As to the vicar, he missed his ass altogether and fell in the bomb hole. Which goes to show . . .' Witchbourne paused dramatically. Tarrou and Turbida seemed frozen, their features pale with insulted sensibility. Only Coote, who was hearing the story for the first time, gave the necessary prompt.

'What?' he asked.

'That the Vicar did not know his ass from a hole in the ground,' said Mitchell Witchbourne with satisfaction. As the waves of unease spread around the table, he gathered up the cards and rose to his feet. 'Beddy bye,' he said softly, disappearing off into the darkness. The others looked at each other with the expression of people who did not know what to think, and did not dare ask.

It was in this atmosphere — a harmony woven of night sounds: the warm darkness beyond the veranda, the tinkle of ice-cubes, the rise and fall of voices — that Bernard Corunna Coote felt impelled to his first confession. Having drunk more than usual one night, he announced, with sudden confidential exactness:

'I am a renegade Protestant!'

There was silence for a moment. Then Witchbourne, who was dealing, flicked an eyebrow upwards. 'Ach so,' he said, in guttural parody.

'We have few Protestants in Central America, as a such,' said Turbida. 'They do not seem to go with the climate.'

'You do not understand,' said Coote, beating the table with his glass. 'I am a renegade Ulster Protestant.'

'I have heard of the Huguenots,' said Tarrou politely. 'And, of course, the Hussites and Lutherans. But I do not know of your sect: is it interesting, perhaps, like the Catharists or Boggomils — Eros rather than Agape?'

'You still do not understand,' said Coote fiercely. 'I am a renegade Ulster Presbyterian; an Orangeman!'

'Ah, a regional form of Calvinism,' said Tarrou sweetly. 'We have had that too: the Jansenists of Port-Royal. But you should not let it worry you.' He studied his cards carefully before raising three fingers. 'Catholics, Protestants, Communists, *nous sommes tous des assassins.*'

A silence fell, heavy as the night outside. It was broken by the sound of Bernard Corunna Coote weeping: one tear fell, with a distinct plop, into his whiskey glass. His large head, flabby with drink, runnelled with tears, looked like a flayed vegetable marrow. The game continued.

After this rash beginning, Bernard Corunna Coote learned to offer his confidences with the same casualness as he played his cards. And though (unlike the latter) they lay without immediate comment, he knew that they were being picked up, one by one, gestures towards a portrait. Assembled, they made what Tarrou once smiling called

LE PETIT TESTAMENT DE BERNARD CORUNNA COOTE.

Bernard Corunna Coote came from a distinguished Ulster family, descendants of Captain William Coote, who was rewarded for his skilful butchery in the Cromwellian campaign with a large grant of Papish land. Industrious in peace as war, he was the founder and first Provost of Strulebridge: an equestrian statue (brave, bettle-browed, a minor hammer of the Lord) still stands in the town square, on the site of an old palace of the O'Neills.

The family seat, however, was at Castlecoote, overlooking the river. At first, little more than a four-square grey farmhouse or 'Bawn' (fortified to prevent the stories of dispossessed Catholic neighbours), it was redesigned by John Nash in 1755. As they watched the new buildings rise — the doorways flanked with fluted Doric columns, the noble rooms with elliptical designs on the ceilings, the terraces diminishing to the river — something seemed to happen to the family features. ('You could see it in the portraits,' said Bernard Corunna Coote, 'they felt easier, less predatory, more secure.')

In this handsome Georgian building, generations of Cootes grew up, the eldest managing the estate (and generally the county as well, being Grand Master of the Orange Lodge), the younger going into colonial service, the daughters marrying other Plantation squires, their equals in land and religion. The only break in this pattern came when war broke out: then, as one man, they rushed to the side of the King. Hardheaded, with the bravery of the Irish, but more sense, they made magnificent soldiers, especially when commanding a regiment of their own tenants. A Coote had led the crucial charge at Corunna, a Coote had been aide-de-camp to Wellington, a Coote had led the Ulster division on the Somme. Whenever the Empire was in danger, a Coote would take command, looking at the battlefield as though it were a few hundred acres of his own land and say, with a brisk return to the vernacular: 'WULL DRIVE THEM THRU THERE!'

To this tradition, compounded of the sword and the ploughshare, was born a son, Bernard Corunna Coote, a sore disappointment. His whole career seemed a demonstration of the principle of cultural reversion, i.e. the invasion of the conqueror by the culture of the conquered. His childhood was spent listening to old Ma Finnegan, the Catholic tenant in the lodge gate: she taught him the Rosary in Irish and the tests for entering the Fianna. His holidays from public school were spent roaming the hills in a kilt, with an Irish wolfhound at his heels. From these walks sprang his vocation: in his third year at Oxford he announced that he was going to be an archaeologist, an expert on the horned cairns of the Carlingford culture, the burial places of the chieftains of Uladh.

He was on a field trip, deciphering standing stones in the Highlands of Donegal, when war broke out in September 1939. Bernard Corunna Coote could no longer resist family tradition: he joined as a volunteer in the North Irish Horse and fought in both the African and Sicilian campaigns. But though he acquitted himself well (whatever else, he was no coward) the contrast between how he regarded himself and what was happening to him became too much to bear. The first his parents heard of it was when he was reported as refusing a decoration 'on the grounds that he did not recognise the present King of England'. A campaign for the use of Gaelic in Irish regiments also brought comment, coinciding as it did with the preparations for D-Day. Invalided out of the army in 1944, he did not (at his father's request) return to Castlecoote. After rattling around Dublin for a few years, he disappeared to America.

III

From these confidences, delivered so haltingly, heard so calmly, Bernard Corunna Coote received the peculiar form of comfort which was the secret of the Hotel Darien. His companions spoke rarely of what he had said (the only direct comment was Tarrou's puzzled remark that he did not see what all this had to do with religion), but he knew that it had been heard, and if not understood, accepted. He became one of the members of an invisible club, an enclosed order whose purpose was not so much contemplative as protective: behind these walls they seemed to say, you are safe, all things are equal, you may live as you like. He no longer sought Hautmoc (Lord High Muck, Witchbourne scornfully called him, his name being that of the last Aztec chieftain who tried to propitiate Cortez by a mass sacrifice) for long conferences, though the latter still watched him from behind the pillars of the arcade as he went to collect his letters. Apart from that morning stroll he had been assimilated into the world of the hotel.

It was some months, however, before he was introduced to the second ritual of the permanent residents: the visit to the town whorehouse. Every Sunday afternoon, led by Mitchell Witchbourne, dazzlingly spruce in white ducks and embroidered shirt, they made their way to an old colonial house at the other end of the town. This spacious building belonged to Doña Anna, a mestizo matron whom Witchbourne — remembering some comic strip of his youth about an orphan girl — had nicknamed Obsidian Annie. She was not really an orphan, but the widow of an officer who had taken the wrong side in the Revolution. Finding herself stranded in San Antonio, she had applied her strong, practical nature to developing the primitive prostitution system of the area — the famous 'double-baths' of festival days — into a regular business. Under her care she had usually about half a dozen young ladies, ranging from sixteen to thirty, with the dusky, almost negroid beauty of the women of the peninsula.

Events at the Casa Anna always followed a definite order, the decorum of Sunday blending with the lady's desire to do her best for her most monied visitors. First, the girls appeared, wearing their holiday best, long flounced skirts, embroidered lace *huipls* or bodices, and heavy ear-rings made out of United States gold pieces. Doña Anna, of course, being one of *los correctos*, the people of good standing, wore a stiff dress of dark Spanish silk, to distinguish herself from such peasant finery. They all had a social drink together while the men made their choice (there was usually a new recruit to spice routine). Then they withdrew to their rooms where, beside each *palias* stood the inevitable bottle of *tequila*. Through the long afternoon everyone loved or drank or watched through the windows the boys shinning the banana trees, like insects on a grass blade. Now and again there was a satisfying plop! as one fell into the undergrowth.

It seemed a good life.

As darkness gathered, everyone came together again for the evening meal. This took place in the dining hall, the largest room in the house, with fortress-like doors opening onto the patio. At the head of the table presided Obsidian Annie, a clapper by her side to summon the two white-coated Indian house boys. As the food piled higher (local delicacies like turtle eggs, or iguana roe, with purple yams and papayas), a kind of wild gaiety seized them, the girls shrieking as the men pinched them through their thin finery. Even Obsidian Annie relaxed her vigilant decorum, growing nostalgic as she drank from the stone jar of fresh *pulque* at her side. Tears trickled down her thick make-up as she remembered the days when she had been a young girl, the great days before the Revolution: Obsidian Annie was not a democrat.

'And on Sunday we all rode together in Chapultepec Park. Oh, you should have seen us, the girls sitting side-saddle, wearing black hats and skirts, and lovely Spanish leather boots. And the men, with their silver buttons and braids, in the *charro* style, as handsome as Cortez!'

It seemed a more than good life.

The delay in introducing Bernard Corunna Coote to the second ritual of the Hotel Darien was cautionary: they feared that the same forces which had pushed him to total confession would push him further, and that they would lose a hard-won recruit. But they need not have worried; he and Doña Anna got on together like a house on fire. Previously it had been Tarrou who had been her favourite, as coming closest to her aristocratic ideal; in moments of tenderness she called him

Maximilian, remembering the blond prince who had tried to bring French civilisation to her country.

But between a suave member of the middle-class and something approaching the real thing, there was no question. In clasping Bernard Corunna Coote to her firmly corseted bosom, she clasped her own youth, a bloated version of the *caballeros* who had escorted her through Chapultepec Park. And from her flatteringly warm embrace (a blend of fustian and volcano), he seemed to extract a maternal solace.

True, he had bouts of restlessness, but they were the 'thick head' of the novice, rather than real rebellion. Whenever he sulked, refusing to come to the banquets by which she set such store, she went to fetch him. Soon they were drinking and singing together, he calling her 'his favourite g-e-l' and teaching her the songs of the Continental Irish brigade:

> On Ramillies field we were forced to yield
> Before the clash of Clare's Dragoons . . .

The only person upset by this arrangement was Tarrou, who discovered in himself vestiges of a jealousy he thought extinct. But having given up life *as a such* (to use Turbida's phrase), why quarrel with one aspect of it? His wit grew more strained, his stories more silkily sadistic, but his ill-humour did not seem to threaten the equilibrium of their communal life. Not, at least, until the night of the May Festival, several months later.

For the members of the Hotel Darien, the May Festival was the major trial of the year, the one day when the town broke in on their consciousness with a usurping rattle and roar. A famous local patriot had said that a Revolution should be as gay as a Carnival: in his memory, San Antonio made its carnivals as violent as revolutions. From the tolling of the cathedral bell in the morning, through the Blessing of the Goats at midday, to the processions in the evening and the Grand Ball at night, it was one long orgy of noise. Indians in gaudy finery pressed through the street, shouting and waving banners: by nightfall most of them were roaring drunk, challenging all comers with their machetes.

In previous years the inhabitants of the hotel had made half-hearted attempts to join in the fun. But they could never relax or feel at home, the locals parting before them as they came to the wooden beer canteens in the square, their connoisseur's interest in the blind flute-player turned to mockery as they passed, the local matrons parting with relief from their embrace in the dance tent, with its flaring gasoline lamps. As they left, they heard the music spring up again, its vitality underlining their isolation:

> Woman is an apple
> Ripe upon a tree —
> He who least expects it
> May have her beauty free;
> And I pray to San Antonio
> *That it may be me!*

Their object became to close it out of their consciousness. They could not go to Doña Anna's establishment because (cupidity getting the better of her aristocratic inclinations), it was full of drunken Indians. Neither could they relax in the garden or on the terrace: the noise was too great. So they remained indoors, with all the windows and doors locked. But the heat became so intense that they felt they were drowning. Even under the fans there was no relief, the metal wings only stirring the thick air.

By nightfall they had gathered in the hotel lounge, in the vague hope of playing their customary game. But they were all drunk, with that peculiar restlessness, that draining of energy which a day's drinking brings. Together with a nervous irritation: Tarrou's voice was razor-sharp with menace.

'Shall we begin now?' he asked, for the third time.

No one spoke. There was a burst of cheering that made the windows rattle. A firework rose in the air, broke and fell, illuminating the room with a sudden glow.

'Shall we begin?' said Tarrou again, rapping the deck of cards on the table.

Still no one spoke. Another firework climbed within the square of the window. Coote watched it moodily: he felt isolated from the others and had the impression he was missing something.

'I see you are impressed by our peasant customs,' said Tarrou, with acidity.

'They do make a lot of noise,' Witchbourne interposed.

'You are not the only one, of course,' continued Tarrou. 'Doña Anna also likes them, although she pretends not to. It is easier to impress peasants.'

'But not so much noise as some city people do,' said Turbida, hastily joining Witchbourne's rescue operations. 'There is a rough night-club behind the Reforma where as soon as the girls appear everyone shouts —' He expired in giggling lecherousness.

But Tarrou was not to be cheated of his prey so easily.

'The noisiest night-club I ever knew was on the borders of the Goutte d'Or district in Paris: you know, the Arab quarter. There was a fat Algerian tout there, a sort of barker. Now that I come to think of it, he resembled our friend here . . .' He gestured towards Coote, who shifted slightly in his chair. Like an animal entering a slaughterhouse, sensing the glint of steel hooks, he was becoming aware of the menace directed towards him.

'The only time there was silence in that club was during the act involving the Siamese twins. Some day I must tell you about that.'

'Some day,' said Witchbourne, gruffly.

'I remember —' said Turbida again.

'But the Siamese twins, though an interesting act, lacked the simplicity, the imaginative daring of the barker's own speciality. I have told you he was an Arab. He wore a long flowing burnous: at first I thought it was for local colour. But at the end of the evening, he removed it, slowly. It was only then that one realised — *on le soupçonne toujours d'ailleurs, avec les types gros comme ça . . .*'

'What?' asked Turbida, in spite of himself.

'That he was a woman. A big, fat, ugly, aged woman.'

There was silence. Mitchell Witchbourne's face was white. But it was Coote who spoke, finally, dragging his great bulk up.

'You go too far,' he said raspingly. 'Even in hell there are limits.'

IV

Happiness is a balance, precariously maintained: to achieve even its semblance requires training. While the others, with instincts geared to survival, swept the incident aside, Bernard Corunna Coote clearly could not. For days he avoided the hotel and news drifted back that he had been seen drinking with Hautmoc. After a while, he began coming again to meals, but when Witchbourne ostentatiously produced the card table he disappeared, and they heard him crunching down the avenue towards the town. He did not even return to the Casa Anna, though Obsidian Annie inquired after him, saying that she had seen him (again with Hautmoc) at the local café.

It was agreed that Tarrou should speak to him. One night, as Coote was ploughing back through the darkness, the slim Frenchman presented himself at the door, his cold eyes taking — but not returning — the latter's surprised glare.

'We do not see you now,' he said pleasantly.

Coote did not answer, all his efforts absorbed in the task of breathing. But he moved forward as though to brush past Tarrou.

'Why do you not join us in the evenings any more?'

Coote stopped. 'You know why.'

'*Mais, mon ami,*' Tarrou spread his hands, gently. 'These things are unimportant. *Dans l'ivresse, comme dans l'amour, il faut tout pardonner.*'

Coote looked at him for a long time, and his eyes seemed to clear in the hallway light. Then he moved forward again, resolutely.

'May mwah, jenny pooh pah,' he said, in his harsh Ulster accent.

For his former companions of the Hotel Darien, however, no answer was final. They did not begin to despair of him even when he disappeared on his first 'expedition'. It looked so harmless, a large man with a morning-after face and stubble, going off into the jungle by himself, carrying a hammer. And the bag of samples he brought back, examining them for hours on the terrace, were like the coloured beads a child might play with. But when instruments and books began to arrive at the post-office and the day's wanderings spread into weeks, they began to be alarmed: in the organised quality of these frenzies, they recognised an alien discipline. Swallowing his pride, Witchbourne went out of his way to speak to Haut-moc, and inquired as to their purpose. The latter graciously accepted the drink offered him, but was far from helpful.

'He is looking for something we have both lost,' he said mysteriously.

Revolver in one hand, machete in the other, his T-shirt moist with sweat (except where the great raft of the sun hat kept a circle of white about his shoulders), he beat his way through the jungle around San Antonio. Behind him followed a retinue of peons, tangle-haired, liquid-eyed, carrying the inevitable burden of impedimenta. With their slow pace, their resigned gestures, they seemed less human beings than like a column of ants, winding its way patiently over and around obstacles.

Even the rainy season did not halt him, physical obstacles being only a drum-call to the military ardours of his ancestry. Coming to a flood-swollen river he would plunge in, his weapons held high above his head: sometimes only the hand and the round circle of the hat could be seen as he sidestroked heavily across. If there was a current he would float with it, until he struck an outcrop. Then, like Excalibur, he broke to the surface and trampled ashore, water dripping from his bulk, as though down the side of a mountain. By the time his followers had crossed (going to a village for the loan of a pirogue, or wading downstream until they found a fording place) he had already blazed a trail into the pelvic rankness of the jungle on the other side.

What the Indians thought of their master — a comic *gringo* if ever there was one — was at first tactfully submerged in the fact that he paid well. Sufficiently well for them to want to humour him when, following some atavistic memory of a Victorian jungle trek, he insisted that they should carry their own packs and leave their burros behind. But as the months passed, something of his anxiety communicated to them: just as they sped with eagerness on his errands, so they watched with increasing concern his disappointment as he turned over the stones they had brought. A man, they knew from their own lives, could only bear so much misfortune: in Bernard Corunna Coote's case they felt that some incongruous struggle was going on, an almost physical rending, as though a blind man were trying to see, or a cripple to walk.

Sometimes he would stop short in his tracks, as if struck by a blow from behind. The pale blue eyes, would glaze and turn inwards, the shoulders hunch, until he looked like the oldest of earth's creatures, some grey mammoth embedded in ice or rock. And the cry that he gave, low at first, rose till it seemed beyond human pitch, a trumpeting that tore the heart with its animal abandon.

It was after one of these outbreaks (dutifully reported by the servants), that the inhabitants of the Hotel Darien decided that a last effort should be made to save Bernard Corunna Coote for themselves. For to their surprise they had discovered that they needed him. From selfish exasperation at the loss of a necessary companion, they had passed to real concern, and an emotion that only their long habits of reticence refused to recognise as love. It was though their bluff had been called, and the suffering they had gradually relegated to the background of their own lives had suddenly reappeared before them, monstrous, dishevelled, wringing its hands.

But what was to be done? They had a formal meeting in the hotel lounge ('the scene of the crime' as Turbida said brightly, before Tarrou's coldly speculative eye fell upon him) to discuss the situation. Tarrou's attempt to apologise had failed. Witchbourne's efforts to elicit information from Hautmoc had been fruitless. There remained Turbida, the soiled innocent of the party, whom no one would ever suspect of any serious motive. Witchbourne's mild eye joined Tarrou's in resting upon him. Turbida must find out what Bernard Corunna Coote thought he was doing.

The opportunity came a few days later when Coote returned from a long absence in the jungle. He looked more exhausted than ever, with a rough growth of beard and a tear in his trousers which exposed long thin legs. But he did not seem surprised to find Turbida in his room, his expensive shape splayed over a cane chair.

'Good day —?' the latter asked, with the upward inflection of the hunting classes.

Bernard Corunna Coote snorted, but did not answer. After depositing a sack in a corner, he dragged off his clothes, and stepped under the shower. Through the yellow curtain Turbida could see his body, a whale under water.

'I have been looking at your books,' shouted Turbida, lifting up a volume, with a large painting of a pyramid on the cover.

Still no answer. The shower sank, a hand groped for a towel: Bernard Corunna Coote emerged, clean, spiky haired, decently clothed in white.

'Interesting chaps, these Aztecs, when you get right down to it,' continued Turbida, turning the pages. 'Place like Monte Alban now, makes you think. . . .'

Coote stopped pummelling himself. 'You have been to Monte Alban?' he asked incredulously.

'Why, yes,' said Turbida, trying desperately to remember the illustrations Tarrou had shown him, 'and to Mitla too.'

'Did you see the scrollwork at Mitla? The cruciform chambers?'

'Yes, yes . . .' encored Turbida.

'The spiral and lozenge pattern are the same as at Newgrange. It was a characteristic of the race, the delight in abstract pattern. But we were a thousand years before.'

Turbida was about to inquire where Newgrange was when he saw that Coote was no longer listening to him, his face contorted with fury and anguish.

'Think of it! When Cortez and his Spaniards came, they found the Maltese cross, and the Indians spoke of strange white men. Certainly it was Brendan —'

'Brendan?' echoed Turbida.

'Saint Brendan who discovered America. But what about even earlier? We know that the Celts were a widely dispersed people: traces of them have been found in Sardinia, Galicia, the valley of the Dordogne. We are the secret mother race of Europe. But if —' he halted, as though transfixed by the daring of this thought.

'If,' prompted Turbida.

'We could prove that the Celts not merely discovered but *founded* America! Think of it —' He brought his face close to that of Turbida, who could smell the furnace blast of cheap spirits.

'Then, for the first time, the two halves of the world would fit together, into one, great, universal Celtic civilisation.' He raised his arms high, then let them fall slowly again. 'All I need is a proof.'

'Like what?' asked Turbida in a hushed voice.

'Oh, there are minor ones. Character for example, Hautmoc says that the original Indians were the purest race in the western hemisphere: we still place a great emphasis on purity. And *physique*; remember the bearded statues of La Venta?' He tugged his own beard vehemently, to emphasise each word. 'After us, there were no bearded men in South America.'

'But a major proof?'

Coote seemed to hesitate. It was months since he had spoken to anyone: should he now reveal his hopes to a comparative stranger? Only the music of international renown could heal several generations of outraged tradition: here, in San Antonio, Bernard Corunna Coote was staging his last fight to restore himself not merely to his family, but to the whole history of human knowledge.

'I told you once of the cairns of Carlingford and the Boyne, the burial places of our early chieftains. From the decorative motifs I deduce a connection between them and the pyramids of the lost civilisations of Central America. But the pyramids, according to Hautmoc, were designed for human sacrifice only, and not for ritual interment. If I could find . . .'

He hesitated again, drew a deep breath.

'Somewhere, in the most remote areas, probably in the thick of the jungle, there must be traces of those earlier structures upon which Monte Alban, Palenque, Chichén Itzá, were based. If I could find one single passage grave or burial chamber . . .'

'Like what? asked Turbida again.

'Like this!' cried Bernard Corunna Coote, seizing and opening a large green volume. 'Look!'

Carlos Turbida was still trembling when he joined the others an hour later.

'But the man is mad,' he cried plaintively.

'The question is irrelevant,' said Witchbourne, with unaccustomed severity. 'Which of us is even half sane?' His gaze swept across his companions, like a searchlight across rocky ground.

'Still, it is strange,' said Tarrou. 'I was sure he was cured. Who would have thought the irrelevant could have such deep roots?'

'But nothing can be done. It is too late . . .' wailed Turbida again.

'It is never too late,' said Witchbourne sententiously. 'While there's life there's hope. What do you think, Tarrou?'

'I think,' said Tarrou, 'that the time has come for our famous reckoning.' From his pocket he produced a sheaf of white dockets, neatly bound with rubber: he ruffled it under their noses.

'A sum of money is always useful,' agreed Witchbourne.

'But then, what will you do?' asked Turbida.

Tarrou struggled. 'We shall see. I will perhaps go and talk to our noble friend, Lord High Muck.'

'But what about?'

'About literature,' smiled Tarrou. 'Where is that book you say Coote gave you?'

V

The rainy season passed. The mouth of the San Antonio River was no longer choked by floating vegetation, and the long dugout canoes could sail directly up to the market place. The mountain paths had dried and the peasants came down to the village in ox-carts, lined with layers of crushed sugarcane. The few meagre crops were to be harvested, maize, sesame seeds, beans. Soon the first tourist bus would turn into the square, to halt for an hour or so before continuing its journey southward.

It was on the anniversary of their first meeting that Hautmoc came to Bernard Corunna Coote with unexpected news. The latter was sitting at his accustomed place on the terrace: he had not been on trek for over a week, and looked more than usually morose, his shoulders slouched over the café table. Behind him hovered the proprietor, fearful not that he would attack anyone (despite his noise, the gross foreigner was surprisingly gentle, not like the common-class of Indians who broke loose with their machetes when drunk) but that he should do himself harm: the day before he had fallen on his way to the lavatory. Now and again, from that seemingly quiescent mound of flesh, a hand would emerge, and grope around the table for the bottle which was poured, with many whistling sighs and groans, in and around his glass.

It was then that Hautmoc appeared on the far side of the square near the post-office. It was hard to miss him because, after several months of unaccustomed prosperity, he had deserted his trampish practices and dressed as befitted a descendant of kings, with an elegant *serape*, slashed in scarlet and black, and a white sombrero. Moreover he was walking briskly, almost running, with an abandon that surprised Bernard Corunna Coote, who had been talking to him only the night before. He came directly to the café table, but did not sit down, gazing at his friend and employer with a kind of tranced look:

'Master,' he said solemnly, 'we may have news.'

Bernard Corunna Coote stirred. 'What do you mean, you may have news?' he grated.

Hautmoc looked over his shoulder, towards the café-owner, indicating that he did not feel free to speak. 'We may have important news,' he repeated.

With an effort, Coote threw out his arm towards the chair opposite him. 'Sit down and have a drink.'

'There is no time,' said Hautmoc. He leaned his head swiftly down towards the other's sunken face, and whispered into his ear: 'We have found what you were looking for.'

Bernard Corunna Coote started. Did Hautmoc know what he was saying? Like the shepherd boy suddenly face to face with the wolf, like the alchemist seeing a yellow liquid condense in his crucible, he gazed at him, slowly believing his eyes.

'Where?' he asked, rising from the table.

The sun was low in the sky on their second day's march when they reached the area indicated by Hautmoc. It lay near the source of the San Antonio River, a region Coote had rarely explored, believing it already well known to the natives. But perhaps he had been wrong to ignore it: after all, river-beds were the traditional centres of civilisation. But so high up? For hours they had climbed up the mountainside, through the thick forest of the lower slopes, where springs made the ground soggy and treacherous. Then they crossed a belt of shale and rock, where the river sank to a trickle, and they found animal skeletons bleaching in the sun. Finally, towards evening, they emerged onto a small plateau set, like a shelf, against the steep incline.

A light wind was blowing. Below them, the valley fell away, a matted sea of vegetation, divided by the thin line of the river. There was no sign of a living thing, the smoke from the occasional village or clearing being absorbed in the transparent mist that lay above the trees. At the limit of their view the sun was sinking, like a coal at the heart of a dying fire.

'Is this the place?' said Bernard Corunna Coote, impatiently.

After easing off their packs, the Indians had gathered around him and Hautmoc, as though waiting for an order. The latter did not answer, but remained looking out, in melodramatic serenity.

'Is this the place?' asked Coote again. 'Where is it, or what is it called?'

'It is called Coatlicue,' said Hautmoc seriously. 'It is one of the most ancient of our sacrificial grounds. The people took refuge here during the Conquest. There used to be a temple.'

'But where —' demanded Coote.

'Behind,' said Hautmoc. Folding his *serape* around him, an elegant figure in scarlet and black, he turned to lead the way.

In his excitement at the view, Bernard Corunna Coote had not yet had time to look behind him. Now, following Hautmoc, he turned. Above them rose a rock face, sheer as a wall, making the area in which they stood seem artificially compact, like an apron stage. The outer edge of the plateau was covered with a hide of tough yellow grass, knotted so close that it made walking difficult. This yielded to a close undergrowth, where lichened boulders lay around like ruins: to Coote's astonishment there was the semblance of a path through it, stained with burro droppings. This led to a clump of well-watered trees: was it the source of the river? Parting the damp oar-shaped leaves, Bernard Corunna Coote saw an open space ahead, a clearing at the entrance of which Hautmoc and his fellow-Indians had gathered to await him.

In the middle of the clearing stood a group of stones. As he drew closer — scattering the natives to right and left like ninepins — he saw that they formed a shape, the unmistakable humped outline of a tumulus. There were two stones on either side, with a closed passage at the far end. There was the great flagstone, resting on the five stones as smoothly as a table top. The whole thing was symmetrical, textbook perfect, even the dark quiet faces grouped around seemed in harmony — except for one thing. As Coote approached, his foot crushed something in the grass. Whoever has hoisted the flagstone had forgotten to remove the pulley rope. It wound imperceptibly down the crevice between the two nearest side stones until, like a snake, its end struck up at the sole of Coote's sandal.

He stood there, looking from the rope to the construction, and back again. Then he followed the rope to its source, under the top stone, and tugged. The stone shifted, audibly. He stepped back and gazed for a long time, until even the Indians — professionals of the steady gaze — felt uneasy. Their leader came over and touched him on the shoulder but Coote did not move.

'Master,' said Hautmoc gently, 'we meant no harm.'

Coote still did not reply, his eye rolling over the same square of space, like an eager student crazed for an answer.

'We would not have known how to build it, but for Señor Tarrou. He taught us. And Señors Witchbourne and Turbida provided the money for the workers.'

Coote looked at him. 'But you, why did you do it? You told me you would have nothing to do with them.'

The dark face of the Indian seemed to crease and open, as though reliving a painful decision.

'They' — he pointed to his fellows around — 'did it because they wished to please you. I —' he hesitated.

'Yes?' demanded Coote.

'I did it because — because if the place you are searching does not exist, then it should. Your dream and mine have much in common.

Coote looked at his companion for a long time. Then a hint of a smile crossed his face.

'Hautmoc,' he said, with majesty, 'you are even madder than I am.'

But the other was not listening, his eyes resting fondly on the stones before him. 'There is still one thing lacking to prove us both right,' he said sadly. 'Such stones cry out to be used.'

For a long time Coote's expression did not change, as if he had not understood what Hautmoc had said. Then he straightened, his great back cracking, and looked at the Indians around. They returned his gaze with expectant, admiring eyes, as though his countenance reflected the pure bronze light of the dying solar god. Knowledge passed swiftly across his face, a spasm of lightning.

'I understand,' he said gravely.

Slowly, with the dignity of a military ceremony, he removed his large sun hat. His face was a hunk of meat, fiery red, but above it his bald head shone, the whitest thing they had ever seen. He stepped briskly forward, the Indians falling in line behind him. When he came to the passage grave he marched straight in, leaving them to file to one side, where the loose rope dangled.

'Pull,' he ordered, settling himself in the trough of red clay. As he waited for the heavens to fall, his countenance became relaxed and pure, all provincial crudity refined to a patrician elegance, the ripe intensity of a soldier leader born of two great traditions. Softly on fields of history, Ramillies and El Alamein, Cremona and the Somme, the warpipes began to grieve. Closing ranks, ghostly regiments listened, Connaught Rangers and Clare's Dragoons, Dublin and Inniskilling Fusiliers, Munsters and Royal Irish, North Irish Horse and Sarsfield's Brigade. The stone started to creak.

'After all, it is a good way for a chieftain to die,' he thought contentedly.